Mary Blount Christian

SEBASTIAN (Super Sleuth) and the Egyptian Connection

Illustrated by Lisa McCue

MACMILLAN PUBLISHING COMPANY
New York
COLLIER MACMILLAN PUBLISHERS
London

To Christopher
(Super Reader)

Text copyright © 1988 by Mary Blount Christian
Illustrations copyright © 1988 by Lisa McCue
Macmillan Publishing Company
866 Third Avenue, New York, NY 10022
Collier Macmillan Canada, Inc.
First Edition
Printed in the United States of America

10   9   8   7   6   5   4   3   2   1

The text of this book is set in 12 pt. Primer.
The illustrations are rendered in scratchboard.

Library of Congress Cataloging-in-Publication Data
Christian, Mary Blount.
Sebastian (super sleuth) and the Egyptian connection.
Summary: Dog detective Sebastian helps his
master find a shipment of stolen Egyptian artifacts
that is being smuggled into the country.
[1. Dogs—Fiction.   2. Smuggling—Fiction.
3. Mystery and detective stories]   I. McCue, Lisa,
ill.   II. Title.
PZ7.C4528Sdd   1988   [Fic]   87-34986
ISBN 0-02-718560-5

Contents

1
What Does a Nose Know?

Sebastian shot a critical sidelong glance at Lady Sharon, Maude Culpepper's Old English sheepdog. The nerve of that bag of fur, lollygagging on *his* favorite spot on *his* couch! A low rumble escaped his fuzzy lips.

"Sebastian!" John yelled from the kitchen, where he and Maude were painting the cabinets. "Enough of that, now. Be a good host."

John Quincy Jones, Sebastian's human, had Sundays off from his job as a city police detective and had decided to give the kitchen a fresh coat of paint. Sebastian, the unofficial but far superior detective, had the day off, too, although he had no intention of spending it painting.

Maude—John called her his girlfriend—had offered to help, though. That was okay, Sebastian figured, but he hated it when John paid more attention

1

to her than to him! And he especially didn't like it when Maude brought Lady Sharon. There was room for only one dog in John's life—and that was the hairy hawkshaw!

Lady Sharon, asleep on the couch, snorted. *Humpf!* Sebastian pouted. Who did she think she was, anyway? Well, she was no *real* competition. Shrugging off thoughts of her like fleas, Sebastian trotted toward the kitchen. How was the painting going? he wondered. And would he approve of the color? It was time he got a look at it.

What was that ladder doing stretched across the kitchen doorway? Well, if he wiggled a little *this* way, then scooted *that* way, he could just make it through. *Ooof!* It was a tighter squeeze than he'd first thought; his flanks were stuck. Sebastian struggled to free himself. The ladder teetered.

"Look out!" Maude shrieked, reaching out too late to steady the ladder.

John, who unfortunately was *on* the ladder, threw up his arms. *Whop!* Gooey sticky paint—azure blue, as it turned out—plopped all over Sebastian's fur.

"Oh, no! Sebastian!" John yelled, scrambling down the ladder.

"Oh, horrors." Maude groaned.

Sebastian wiggled free of the ladder and shook. Blue paint splattered all over Maude, John, the cabinets, and the newspapers that John had spread on

the floor to protect the linoleum. Now Sebastian was really in trouble!

Quickly he slumped into a hangdog position and whimpered pitifully, rolling his eyes. That always got to John. He couldn't fuss at such a winsome canine, could he?

"Stay there on those papers and don't move a muscle!" John commanded. He grabbed a can of turpentine and a couple of rags. John tossed one of the rags to Maude, who dabbed at the paint on the appliances while he tried to clean up Sebastian.

Phew! That stuff smelled awful, and it made Sebastian's eyes water.

"I guess that's about as clean as I can get you," John muttered, just as Sebastian was about to give up hope. "Now, you stay right there on those papers," he told Sebastian.

Turning toward Maude, John asked, "How about some pizza? I've got a couple in the freezer and can pop 'em in the oven real quick."

"Sounds great," Maude told him. "I'll make some coffee. And should I feed the dogs something? Do you have any dry dog food here?" She peeked inside a couple of cabinets as she spoke, retrieving a jar of instant coffee.

"No," John said, "and it's the strangest thing, too. I know I buy it, but I can never find it when I want it."

Actually, there was nothing strange about it. John brought it in, and Sebastian dragged it out through the doggie door to the bird feeder. He hoped John would eventually get tired of bringing the yukky stuff home.

"I guess they can have a little of the pizza. It's got meat and cheese and stuff like that," John suggested.

Now he was talking! All that *good* stuff!

While John was baking the pizza and making a tossed green salad for himself and Maude, Sebastian entertained himself by reading the newspapers spread around him. Might as well read; sitting was so boring. Besides, it was the only thing he could do without getting into trouble. *Hmmm.* The Tigers had won another football game, the headline said. Who'd want to name a team after cats, even big ones? There was a story about some city councilman griping about a new sculpture put in front of City Hall. It was pretty silly looking. Sebastian belly-crawled to another page. John had told him to stay still, but surely he hadn't meant for him to read the same page over and over. What was that weird picture?

Cautiously Sebastian leaned forward to get a closer look. It was a house that looked like a pyramid, stuck right in the middle of a neighborhood. The picture showed neighbors marching in front of it with protest signs. "It's un-American," an unidentified neighbor complained. "Why couldn't he build Greek Revival or French Provincial like the rest of us?"

Sebastian read on: "Carmine Rothwi . . . "—there was a blob of blue paint blocking the rest of the name— "has announced he will show off his home, which is decorated throughout with replicas of Egyptian artifacts and household furniture at . . . " That was blotted out with paint, too.

"Pizza's served. You can get up now, Sebastian," John said.

Wiggling with delight, Sebastian hurried to his plate to get his pizza. But what a shock! He couldn't smell it! All he could smell was that turpentine. And since he couldn't smell the pizza, he could barely taste it. Sighing, he ate, anyway, assuring himself that he must be enjoying it. After all, he always had before.

While they were eating, the phone rang. John answered. "Hasan! Hasan, is it really you?" He cupped his hand over the phone and quickly told Maude, "It's Hasan el-Salim, my Egyptian friend."

Sebastian jumped onto the couch and glared at Lady Sharon until she moved over. He'd heard about Hasan before. He was a detective in Alexandria, Egypt, and had trained with John at the police academy. The city often let some of their police train in a foreign country, and that country sent a few of its own police to train in the city. That way they could learn each other's methods of detection and maybe pick up new ideas to take home.

John and Hasan had become the best of friends. That was before Sebastian and John had met, of course.

"We'll meet you there. See you then!" John hung up, excited. "It'll be wonderful to see Hasan again. He's coming on a case, but he didn't want to discuss it over the phone. He's going to ask Chief for my help," he told Maude. Chief was John's (and, indirectly, Sebastian's) boss, a beetle-browed grouch of a man.

John was forgetting all about *him* again. What help could John be without his fuzzy partner?

But, wait a minute! What about his sense of smell? That pizza might as well have been crushed concrete, for all he could tell. How would he manage to sniff out clues?

2
A Glimmer of Hope

Sebastian awoke the next morning to the sound of sizzling bacon and eggs. But he could barely smell them. And his nose felt tender, too. Disappointing. But then, if he had a little sense of smell back now, surely the rest would return soon. He trotted into the kitchen, carefully avoiding the new paint. He didn't want to get turpentined again!

John was whistling under his breath. He seemed really happy this morning. Sebastian remembered that it was because of Hasan.

While Sebastian ate his own breakfast of chopped beef, cheese, and eggs, John called Chief. "I'll be a little late this morning, Chief. I'm supposed to pick up Detective el-Salim at the airport. You remember Hasan from academy days, don't you, Chief? He did talk to you from the airplane first thing this morning, didn't he?"

John paused, listening, then said, "Chief, he didn't ask for me to be assigned to the case with him just because we're friends. . . . No, sir, I'm *not* going to be in the way." John hung up and made a face. "Why can't Chief give me any credit?" he muttered.

Sebastian knew exactly how John felt! *He* didn't get any credit, either. And if there was anyone Chief liked less than John, it was Sebastian.

It was around ten in the morning when John and Sebastian went to the airport. The big Egypt Air plane was just landing.

By the time John had found a parking space, Hasan was emerging from the customs area with his luggage. John rushed to embrace the slender, dark-eyed man with the wide smile.

"John, my friend, time has been good to you," Hasan said. He pulled back and looked at Sebastian. "Ah, and this must be the fine animal you described in your letters. Sebastian, you said?"

John had written Hasan about him? He must have been quite complimentary, from what Hasan said. The cuddly canine blushed right through the fuzz on his face.

Hasan offered his hand, palm up, in a gesture of goodwill. Sebastian nuzzled it. Then Hasan scratched Sebastian behind the ears and became an instant friend.

Sebastian trotted alongside Hasan and John, eavesdropping.

"So, what's this case all about, Hasan?" John

asked as they strolled toward the car. "I can't imagine what sort of case would bring you all the way to our part of the world, unless, of course, you're working on a smuggling case."

"Ah, my friend, John, as sharp as ever," Hasan said.

Sebastian sniffed indignantly. He'd been just about to guess that himself.

John, Hasan, and Sebastian went straight to Chief's office. Chief leaned across his desk to shake hands with Hasan, glare at John, and snarl at Sebastian. "Welcome back to America, Detective el-Salim. John, why are *you* here? Don't you dare eat my diet salad, you four-legged garbage disposal."

Hasan smiled at Chief as he spoke. "I have asked my friend John to work with me—with your permission, naturally. We work together so well, you understand."

Chief walked around to the front of his desk. "Hmmm, yes, certainly—if you don't think he and that fleabag will get in the way. So tell me why you are here, Detective el-Salim." He motioned for them to sit down.

Sebastian broke into a panting grin and slid closer to Chief's "diet" salad. He may not have had all of his sense of smell back, but he could see calorie-dripping dressing, fat chunks of cheese, and strips of juicy ham. Not very dietetic, actually. He inhaled the aromas, which were now only slightly tainted with turpentine.

"I am in search of smugglers who have taken some of our national treasures." Hasan pulled photos from a file folder and spread them over the desk. "Priceless treasures from the tomb of Snoferu."

"Snoferu?" Chief said. "I thought his name was Toot or Tuf or—"

"Tutankhamen?" Hasan said. "Egypt had many kings in its history. Snoferu is not as well known as the boy king, of course. But his treasures belong to Egypt, all the same, and they are just as rare and precious."

Fourth dynasty, wasn't it? Sebastian wondered, searching his keen mind. He'd read all about that. Yes, first king of the fourth, he recalled.

"Snoferu was the first king of the fourth dynasty," Hasan said, confirming the hairy hawkshaw's memory. "Look for yourselves at these photographs. They reveal the exquisite craftsmanship of a past life— irreplaceable sculptures and artifacts."

Sebastian stretched his neck to see. There were lots of pretty pieces made of gold and turquoise and shiny white or black rocklike stuff. *Ikk!* One piece was a black cat with eyes of green-colored glass and a turquoise collar. Poor ancient Egyptians: They had no Old English sheepdogs to brighten their lives. But cats? Really! Sebastian squinted at the typed

11

description under the picture. It said the statue was made of onyx, which must be that black stuff. The white stuff, then, must be the alabaster the description mentioned. He did regret he hadn't studied geology more. He made a mental note to correct that next time John went to the library.

Some of the pieces were solid gold. One was a ceremonial mummy mask with colored glass designs on it; another was a statue of a cobra with its hood spread out. There were other gold pieces, too: rings, bracelets, carved cups, and boxes.

Hasan pointed to the photo of a running deer carved from ivory and painted gold. "This is a whip handle," he said. "And this lion's head is from a solid-gold bed," he told them.

Beautiful, Sebastian thought. As beautiful as a dog's cold nose on a summer's day. They belonged to the world, not some miserly old thief. He had to find them and help Hasan return them to Egypt.

"These priceless pieces were in the basement of our museum in Cairo waiting to be cataloged and prepared for display, when they were stolen. I managed to track the thieves and the artifacts to a warehouse in Alexandria. But, alas, I was alone. I was able to handcuff two of them to metal posts, but I was then overwhelmed by the other two. They not only avoided capture, but also left the two handcuffed thieves behind, demonstrating their poor character. They got away with the—how do you say?—goods. It was two days before my men found us there," Hasan said.

Alexandria, Egypt, Sebastian recalled, had a shipping port, as well as airports. And, of course, it had postal services, too.

"By the time I was released from the hospital and able to obtain the necessary papers and funds to come here in pursuit, they had gotten five more days' head start on me. If they used a cargo plane to bring in the artifacts, they may have beaten me here," Hasan said.

"Naturally we questioned the captured men at length. Their testimonies seemed to agree that *your* city is to be the recipient of the artifacts," Hasan told John and Chief. He brightened. "And I have reason to believe they are bringing the artifacts by sea. One of those who got away had a tattoo on his arm; it was of a ship. I think he is a sailor. Besides, one of his captured cohorts practically admitted this."

Sebastian nodded admiringly. Hasan had noticed the ship tattoo—not bad detective work.

Hasan cupped his head in his hands. "I let these beautiful treasures from our past slip through my fingers. I have failed my country miserably. I must find them. I must."

Sebastian ached for Hasan. While he, himself,

had never failed in a task, he could imagine how horrible it would feel.

Hasan pressed his lips together and narrowed his gaze before speaking again. "During the struggle with the thieves, my gun fired accidentally, and I hit several of the packing cases. I feel certain that the spent bullets lodged in the thick packing material surrounding the stolen pieces. The thieves did not examine the cases after I was tied up, and if they did not repackage the pieces . . ."

John leaped to his feet. "We'll alert the port customs inspectors immediately. They have several teams of dogs trained in sniffing out gunpowder. We'll notify the airport and postal securities, too, just in case that tattoo meant nothing."

Good work. John was covering all the angles, just as the old hairy hawkshaw would. But they shouldn't depend on those strange dogs! A sensitive nose was a gift! Those dogs were taught to respond to just one odor, and they were trained like a bunch of senseless puppies at that! The trainer would soak their toys in the odor, then allow them to play only when they had detected that odor hidden away!

Most of the dogs were trained to smell a specific drug or perhaps plastique explosive or gunpowder. But because of illegal-weapons exporting, officers were now training some dogs to react to the smell of the packing grease used to coat the weapons during transport. Generally, the dogs worked in teams—one an expert in gunpowder and the other a specialist in packing grease. They checked outgoing cases, while a team of drug-sniffing dogs worked the incoming material.

Now, he, Sebastian (Super Sleuth), had the ability to distinguish a full range of smells, and not from playing silly games, either. It was a natural ability, for which he was grateful to his mother and father.

Sebastian moved closer to Chief's salad and sucked up the strips of ham. *Ummm.* He slurped up the cheese. Only the hairy hawkshaw could detect the difference between fine mozzarella cheese and Monterey jack—until the terrible turpentine incident, that is.

"Then it's settled, Detective el-Salim," Chief said. "We'll alert the customs folks right away. You will have at your disposal any of our men and dogs. Are you sure you don't want some *other* detective? Hey! That walking garbage can ate my diet salad!"

Sebastian licked his lips. Correction, Chief. The "diet" part, the lettuce, was still intact. He'd actually done Chief a favor, getting all that fat stuff out! The cagey canine trotted out the door ahead of John and Hasan, eager to get away from Chief's nasty glare.

But mostly he was anxious to get to work on the case. Smugglers, beware, for Sebastian (Super Sleuth) was on the job now!

3
Scent-illating Crime

As they hurried from the police station, Sebastian stuck close to Hasan, listening to everything he had to say. The hairy hawkshaw's keen ears and eyes, his superintelligence—these would serve him well until his nose regained its full abilities.

"Do you think someone will ask for ransom?" John asked, voicing a question that was racing through Sebastian's mind, too. These thieves might figure the Egyptian government would be willing to pay lots of money for the return of the artifacts.

"We have not ruled that out, of course. But we think otherwise," Hasan replied. "Had they wished just to hide the items away, the hills are dotted with caves. They would not have had to chance being caught while transporting the pieces."

"What if they melted the pieces down?" John said. "We'd never find them."

Hasan shook his head. "Gold is still valuable. But turquoise is common, as are glass and stones. The pieces are valuable for what they are—ancient relics, an artistry gone forever."

"But what else could anyone do with them?" John blurted out. Sebastian was so proud of him. He was asking all the right questions.

"You would be surprised, my friend, at the number of museums in the world that are displaying ill-gotten pieces of our past. And then, there might be very rich private collectors who enjoy having rare bits of history around them."

"But what's the use of having artifacts if you can't show them off?" John wanted to know.

Hasan shrugged. "Perhaps displaying the artifacts isn't as important to these possibly eccentric persons as owning them. Or perhaps they like the excitement of knowing that tucked away in some dark vault are pieces coveted by many, pieces that are priceless and unique. Maybe they will stay hidden for many years until, as you say, the heat is off."

Sebastian's mouth watered. That made sense. He could understand the excitement of having something tucked away, something coveted by others. Think of all those lovely bones he had buried around the yard. It was exciting to know that they were hidden, and that plenty of dogs—including Lady Sharon—would love to get their paws on them. But why want something you couldn't chew or eat or sleep in?

"We believe that the smuggler must be a private collector who has hired thieves to steal the pieces," Hasan said. "I am afraid that once the artifacts reach that person, they will be lost. Therefore it is most important that we find them at the port, before the thieves can deliver the stolen pieces."

Sebastian sighed wearily. The port was a big place. Ships were stacked up in the channel, waiting to get a berth on the dock and be unloaded and reloaded. Fishermen and shrimpers had to weave their way through all the ships just to bring their catches in for sale. And how would the pieces be packed? Hasan had said in boxes with protective insulation. He hadn't mentioned any labels on the boxes, however.

"Hasan, were the boxes that you hit with your bullets marked in any way?" John asked, once more voicing Sebastian's own thoughts.

"There were no marks," Hasan said. "They could be labeled by now, however. The boxes might say anything. They might even have been exchanged for other boxes. In that case, we are lost, we are lost." Hasan sounded frantic, and his face seemed to wilt.

"Now, don't worry, Hasan," John told him. "We're on the case together now."

Was John finally giving Sebastian the credit he so deserved?

"Yessir, Hasan, with you and me working together the way we did in the police academy, nobody's getting away with this!" John finished.

Humpt! Sebastian mulled over what he knew. The pieces would be heavy, very heavy. And they could come labeled as anything from tools to straw hats, and in boxes of a variety of sizes. They might even have been hidden away in the trunk of a car. Or shipped in the bowels of an oil tanker. How could the police check every single box in every single ship coming in from Egypt? It seemed an impossible task.

"I'm going to drop Sebastian off at the house," John told Hasan when they reached the car. "I hate to leave him at home, since he gets into so much trouble without supervision. But he'd just be in the way at the port. I don't want him getting into any scuffles with the customs dogs."

Trouble? What trouble? Was John still miffed because he'd chewed the corner off the welcome mat? If *that* bothered John, maybe he shouldn't have dropped the jar of barbecue sauce on the mat when he was carrying in the groceries.

What a rotten trick, taking him home. But getting away from home would be as easy as barking. Nobody kept this crime hound out of the action!

4
A Nose for News

Sebastian whimpered woefully as John shoved him into the house. He didn't want John to think he approved of being dumped just as the case got hot.

"Here," John said, hurriedly shoving a milk bone toward Sebastian. "Have a yummy bone. That should make up for being left behind."

Humpt! Not even a real bone. Still, he *was* hungry. He snapped the bone and chomped, swallowing it before the lock on the door clicked.

Sebastian ran to the window and rose up on his hind legs. He pressed his nose to the window and watched. As soon as John's brown car had disappeared around the corner, he dashed through the doggie door and down the sidewalk.

John and Hasan would have the port covered for now. And Hasan was familiar with the stolen relics. Sebastian, on the other hand, had no idea as to the actual sizes of those statues and jars. Then Sebastian remembered the newspaper article about the man who had built himself a pyramid with replicas of Egyptian artifacts and furnishings. Maybe if he got a close look at those fakes he'd have a better idea of what he was looking for. But the paint had obscured part of the owner's name.

Maybe if he slipped into the newspaper office he could find a copy of the story without blue paint. Sebastian trotted to Polk and Travis, where the *City Clarion* building was located. He waited outside until a woman with a camera rushed into the building, and then he went in, too.

Ah, luck was with the old hairy hawkshaw. He saw an open closet behind the receptionist's desk. Since she was too busy reading the comics to notice him, he crept inside and found he had his pick of hats and coats. He wiggled into a trench coat and a battered old felt hat with a pencil and a card in its band that said PRESS PASS.

The receptionist glanced up and nodded at Sebastian as he headed through the swinging door and into the newsroom. Word processors made little clicking noises while reporters hovered over them, typing. A couple of reporters were yelling into phones. They were all too busy to notice a stranger in their midst.

Sebastian spotted the library. Many years ago he'd read somewhere that it was called the morgue. Whatever it was called, that would be where he'd find the story.

The paper John had had on the floor was at least

a week old. Sebastian had little hope of finding an old copy of the paper lying around. But he'd done research with John before. He remembered that the newspaper didn't keep clippings of stories anymore. Instead it stored all the stories in computer files.

In the library Sebastian saw several computers lined up against a wall. A huge poster on the wall said: TO USE YOUR LIBRARY COMPUTERS STRIKE GOTO KEY THEN TYPE IN KEY WORDS. That seemed easy enough. But the keys were so little, and his paws were so big! How could he work that machine?

The keen canine mind was never at a loss for long! Sebastian clutched a pencil between his teeth and tapped out the message: GOTO PYRAMIDS. The screen said: ANCIENT OR MODERN? Sebastian moved the cursor to MODERN, then struck EXECUTE.

Sebastian couldn't imagine two men building themselves pyramid houses, but the machine brought up two stories. He dismissed the first one, since that family was in another city. Ah, there it was, the whole story without paint blobs: Mr. Carmine Rothwinger had decided to open his house to the public to "satisfy its curiosity," he said. Then he'd close it forever to public view.

The story went on to say that he was very wealthy and owned several businesses. In his pyramidlike house, he had copies of many of the chairs, tables, and statues found in the tomb of King Tut and other

pharaohs. There was a picture of Mr. Rothwinger holding a walking staff, sort of a long cane, with the image of King Tut carved on its handle. His fingers were covered with rings, some of them not unlike those Sebastian had seen in Hasan's photos. He said the originals were gold, but his were brass. "I love everything ancient Egyptian," he said.

The free open house would be May first. Sebastian glanced at the calendar on the wall. That was today!

He dashed from the library, through the newsroom, and out the door. What a perfect opportunity to get into the house and examine Mr. Rothwinger's pieces. That way the cunning canine would have a more accurate idea of the size of the real ones.

The story had said the house was on Buttercup Lane, and that you couldn't miss it. How right it was! Everywhere on Buttercup Lane, cars were honking and creeping along as passengers hung out their windows and gawked at the weird place. Pedestrians were lined up around the block, shuffling along the sidewalk and through the gate. There it was—a pyramid, right before his eyes.

Sebastian didn't want to get at the end of the line. Detectives hardly had time to waste. Maybe he could slip through. He slumped under the trench coat and hat and crawled along the wall.

"Hey, you!" a man in a security uniform yelled.

Sebastian cringed. Had they found him out?

5
To See the Sea

Sebastian held his breath, awaiting the moment when the man would rip off his press clothes and reveal his true identity. But the guard smiled at him and waved him through. "Reporters don't have to wait," the man said. "Mr. Rothwinger wants all the reporters he can get. Go on in."

Sebastian nodded gratefully as he sauntered past the crowd and through the front door, which oddly enough looked fairly normal. Inside, the rooms didn't look too weird, either, except that the walls leaned in. Everywhere were relics like those he'd seen in Hasan's photos: animal statues, jars, vases, some life-size statues of people, a chair that looked like a throne, and, in the bedroom, a bed with a lion's head on each corner. The bed must be a replica of the one Hasan had said was stolen.

Mr. Rothwinger was prancing around in a gold lamé outfit that looked fit for an Egyptian king. He was waving his hands around so that the rings on his fingers caught the light. Fakes, definitely fakes.

"The alabaster items are really plaster of paris," Mr. Rothwinger said, turning a spread-winged bird upside down to show its chalky bottom. "And the gold-looking things are brass, not even gold plate. The ebony is just painted that way. And the glass beads are machine made. I'm afraid I'm just a big fake!" He chuckled so that his stomach rolled. "I love *everything* Egyptian." He seemed proud of all his phony stuff.

A man in a gray pin-striped suit backed into Sebastian. Instead of apologizing he sneered, crossing his arms across his chest.

"Ah, do I recognize Goodson Wittman, the prominent curator of the fine arts museum?" Mr. Rothwinger gushed. He rushed over, offering a be-ringed hand to the man.

Goodson Wittman didn't take his hand. "I just had to see for myself, Rothwinger. Unbelievable. Simply unbelievable."

"Yes, yes, you like it," he said, nodding.

"I didn't say that! I only said it was unbelievable," Wittman said. "How do you live in this uncomfortable place?"

"Like the pharaohs, dear Wittman," Rothwinger

said. "Like the pharaohs. But, of course, you have many fine Egyptian pieces in your museum." Rothwinger raised his voice slightly. "Not all of it there, shall we say, ummm, legally, ummm?"

Wittman squared his shoulders and jammed his hands into the pockets of his coat. "Almost all museums have such pieces, Rothwinger! We are actually doing countries a favor, preserving their history for them in constant temperatures and favorable light. We—"

Rothwinger glanced around the room as if making sure he had everyone's attention. "Ah, yes. The kindly curator, stealing for the good of others."

Goodson Wittman's face was red, and his eyes seemed to pop from his face. "I do not steal, Rothwinger! I have accepted, er, questionable property, and I'd do it again if I could. We give people the opportunity to see *real* artifacts, not cheap imitations like—"

Rothwinger clasped his hands together. "Yes, yes. They are cheap, and they are imitations. I bow to your expert opinion."

Sebastian was shocked! Why, the man was nothing better than a thief! And he said he'd do it again. Had *he* stolen Hasan's treasures?

A man in white gloves and a suit with tails came in, and Mr. Rothwinger bent to let the man whisper in his ear. He went pale momentarily, but seemed to straighten up. "Gentlemen, gentlemen, do come in. The police, you say?"

It was John and Hasan! They must have had the same idea as he about looking at the replicas. Sebastian jumped, knocking a bowl resembling a lotus cup from a pedestal. It crumbled into powdery chips of plaster of paris. He stood frozen next to the debris, waiting for Rothwinger to yell at him.

Instead, Mr. Rothwinger just laughed. "Not to worry." He dismissed it with a wave of his be-ringed fingers. "As I said, it's merely a cheap copy. There are more where that came from. Don't want to make the press mad. Do you have everything you need?"

Sebastian moved away, trying to keep his back to John and Hasan. What if they recognized him in spite of his disguise? John never had, of course, but what if he *did* someday? He'd be awfully angry! Mr. Rothwinger hadn't yelled at him, but John would!

He scooted past the guards and into the street, hurrying back to the newspaper office to leave the hat and coat before they were missed.

And just in time, too! No sooner had he returned the clothing to the closet and started out than a man with a mustache reached for the hat and coat. "Hey!" he yelled at the receptionist. "How'd my hat get dog fur in it? It was just hanging there in the closet. And look at my coat!"

She rolled her eyes. "Well, everybody says you go

after news like a dog after a fox!" Her shoulders shook as she sniggered.

Sebastian's lips parted in a panting laugh. But enough of this levity. There were smugglers at large! With a better idea about the size of the pieces, he felt it was time to look through the dock area.

Sebastian trotted along the row of warehouses that lined the docks. Fat little fishing trawlers bobbed up and down in the waves, bumping against the dock. Big ships were moored alongside the dock, where handpainted numbers announced their assigned spaces. A conveyer belt was pushed against one, and huge boxes marked FRAGILE/BANANAS were being lowered to the dock from an opening in the side of the ship.

Sebastian's knowledge of the shipping industry wasn't extensive, unfortunately. He figured it would be a good idea to watch for a while.

Each ship he saw had its own name and the name of its owner painted on the bow, he noted. Too bad the print didn't tell where it was coming from, too!

Longshoremen were grabbing the boxes with big hooks and heaving them into trucks. A man stood close by, pointing at one box, then another. The boxes were opened, and the man poked at the banana clusters inside, then waved them away.

Edging closer, Sebastian saw that the man wore a badge that said HEALTH INSPECTOR. There were no dogs sniffing those boxes. And the man looked inside only one out of every hundred or so. How alarming! Why, anything could be in the other boxes.

He crept close to one of the boxes and inhaled deeply. There was a strong banana scent. At last his sense of smell seemed completely intact. Now that he was closer, Sebastian could see smaller print on the boxes. It said Honduras. Wasn't that in Central America? No danger of the artifacts being in one of those packages. But what if the inspectors checked only a few boxes shipped from Alexandria? The artifacts could slip right through their—

"Hey!" a man with hairy arms and big ears yelled. "Get away from there, you mangy mutt!" A hook sailed past Sebastian's left ear and stuck in one of the boxes. "Somebody call the dogcatcher!"

Yipping, Sebastian dashed among the forest of legs and down the dock, leaping onto the deck of a fishing trawler. He could hide among the many ice chests on board until the man quit looking for him. *Phew!* This place certainly smelled fishy.

Sebastian crouched there for what must have been five minutes. And all the while, sea gulls, attracted by the smell of the fish, circled overhead, screaming and diving dangerously close to his fuzzy body. *Shoo!*

One ear cocked, he listened. Footsteps were com-

ing! He tensed his muscles, ready to run. A man with a sunburned, weatherbeaten face reached over and heaved one ice chest to his shoulder. His eyes widened. "Hello, poochie. You want to be an old sea dog, maybe?" He laughed as he stepped off the boat and put the chest on the dock.

He stepped back on deck and heaved another chest to his shoulder. "Maybe you better go before the captain sees you, poochie. We gotta sell our fish and shrimp while it's fresh, you know," he told Sebastian. "Here he comes now with some buyers. Run on."

Gratefully, Sebastian scooted off the boat and past the captain and some other people. They were probably restaurant people. That seafood would be on customers' platters tonight.

And speaking of tonight, he had better get home before John did.

As he trotted home, he thought about the artifacts. It had been two days before Hasan was found by his men. He had been in the hospital another day. Then it had taken two days for Hasan's travel request to be reviewed and approved by his superiors, and another two days before he had gotten the money from his department accountant.

If the artifacts were coming by ship, and the ship made stops along the way, it could be a month before they arrived in port. But if the ship was fast and had no delays, Sebastian figured the artifacts would arrive tomorrow at the earliest. Maybe he could find out if any ships were coming from Alexandria in the next few days. The next day's arrivals and departures of ships were always in the newspaper on the business pages. He could check there before dinner. On second thought, *after* dinner. He was starving!

Sebastian had just dashed through the doggie door and settled himself on the couch when John got home.

John walked through all the rooms, then returned, smiling. "Good dog! I can't find anything broken or torn. What a good dog you've been! Come, boy. Hasan is in the car, waiting. We're having dinner at Maude's. Come!"

Maude met them at the door. "I hope you all like fish!" she said. "I've fixed blackened redfish, boiled potatoes, and slaw."

Fish? *Ikk!* After smelling the port today, he was not all that enthusiastic about fish. It may have been Sebastian's imagination, but he thought he saw a flicker of the same feeling on the faces of John and Hasan.

"Any luck on your case?" Maude asked as she set the table.

"Not really," John said. "We're checking all of the ships coming from the Middle East or from connections with ships from the Middle East. Maybe something will turn up."

"Yes," Hasan said, sighing wistfully, "we are not overlooking the possibility that the artifacts might have changed ships. So many ships to check, it is like your saying about looking for a needle in a haystack."

Sebastian echoed Hasan's sigh. Detective work was like that. You had to turn over a lot of hay before you found the needle. And you had to examine a lot of clues before you found the solution.

Maude invited them to sit down at the table. "I've picked the bones out of some redfish for the dogs to eat, so let's dig in."

While they ate—the humans at the table, and Sebastian and Lady Sharon on the floor in the kitchen—Sebastian reviewed the clues:

Most of the Egyptian artifacts stolen from the Cairo museum basement were small enough to be concealed in cases about the size of bread boxes. The arrested thieves had indicated that the pieces were bound for this city. But what was their final destination? Hasan had said some museums would take stolen artifacts. That Goodson Wittman from the art museum seemed a likely suspect. He had said he would take stolen artifacts, if he could get them! Or the artifacts might be going to a private, eccentric collector. Rothwinger was a collector, and he certainly could be called eccentric. But he was satisfied with replicas.

Ransom seemed an unlikely motive. No one had contacted the Egyptian museum. And, as Hasan said, if the thief wanted ransom, he wouldn't bring the pieces here.

Sebastian slurped the last of his fish, and since Lady Sharon had abandoned a bit on her plate, he ate that, too. He was doing her a favor; fish couldn't be saved.

The humans had eaten and cleared the table, and they were talking in the living room, laughing about John and Hasan's days at the police academy.

Sebastian was free to snoop for the morning newspaper. He found it folded in a basket. He nosed and pawed at it, finally opening it to the shipping news.

The chart said DEP and ARR—that must mean departures and arrivals. He wasn't interested in what was going out, only in what was coming in. It said ARR: 12n/frm: AlexE/Cleopatra/CarmLn/olives/olive oil/dates/B42. That must mean arrival at twelve noon. AlexE had to mean Alexandria, Egypt. And probably the ship's name was *Cleopatra,* and it would be carrying olives, olive oil, and dates. B42—that must be Berth 42. But what did CarmLn mean?

There was a second listing that caught Sebastian's eye: ARR: 3p/frm: AlexE/Bastet/CarmLn/dates/souv'rs/B38. That must mean arrival at three P.M. from Alexandria, Egypt, a ship called *Bastet*—Se-

37

bastian curled his lip at that. Wasn't Bastet the Egyptian cat goddess? How could anybody name a ship after a cat? *Ikk!* It was carrying dates and souv'rs—could that be souvenirs? A perfect cover for the real thing! And the berth would be 38.

But there was CarmLn again. What was that? His keen eyes scanned the page until he spotted a key to abbreviations. CarmLn—Carmine Ship Lines. Carmine. . . . Wasn't Mr. Rothwinger's name Carmine? The news article had said he had several businesses. And he himself had said he loved everything Egyptian. Was that why two of his ships were coming from Egypt? Were they bringing him more phony artifacts? Or might the *real* artifacts be aboard? What a perfect setup!

Now to let John know, so he wouldn't have to be watching the entire dock. He grabbed the newspaper to take to John. But that silly Lady Sharon thought he was playing! She grabbed the other end of the paper and tugged with all her might. Sebastian tugged back, growling. This was no time to be a gentleman.

Unfortunately, it only encouraged Lady Sharon to continue her silly game. She growled deep in her throat and held on tightly. Sebastian weighed more, and he was the stronger of the two. So he simply pulled her along with him as he made his way to John and Hasan.

Lady Sharon would have none of this. When Sebastian had almost reached John, she braced herself and yanked hard. *Rrrrrpt!* The paper tore, and Sebastian found himself holding the wrong half.

"Sebastian!" John yelled, grabbing for the ruff around his neck. "No!"

Groaning, Sebastian wiggled free of John's grasp, dropping the piece of paper he held to snap at the one Lady Sharon clutched between her teeth. *Rrrrrpt!* It tore again.

"Naughty!" John yelled, grabbing the paper from Sebastian and at the same time snatching the piece from Lady Sharon. He wadded up the papers and hurried into the kitchen. Sebastian heard the sickening sound of the heavy lid of Maude's kitchen garbage pail clanging shut.

So much for Plan A. He'd just have to go to Plan B. Whatever *that* was.

6
For Two Scents

Sebastian's mind raced while John was driving Hasan to the hotel, then driving home. He finally decided he'd just have to solve the case by himself. So what else was new?

Fortunately, the two ships would dock at widely spaced times. And they would be only four berths apart. That would give him the opportunity to examine the contents of both.

But he would need a disguise. What should he be? A sailor? That would enable him to board the ships and prowl unnoticed among the holds and corridors. Remembering the way the fishing trawler had bobbed up and down and the way those frantic birds kept diving and screaming, he gulped uneasily. Was going aboard really necessary?

"Come along, Sebastian," John interrupted. "Into the house and to bed with you. I really must say that I was disappointed in you tonight, fighting with Lady Sharon over a newspaper, littering Maude's living room with scrap paper. Now, not another peep out of you, old fellow."

Sebastian tucked the stub of his tail close to his body and slunk into the house, trying to look hangdog.

He crept onto the couch and curled himself into a tight ball. He watched John out of the corner of his eye.

"That's better," John said. "Good-night, boy." He turned the light out.

Sebastian's head popped up, and he peered over the couch arm. The bedroom door was shut. Good, John was out of the way. Now the old super sleuth could think things through uninterrupted. The sailor disguise was unappealing, although he would use it in an emergency. Perhaps he could disguise himself as a longshoreman. In overalls, with maybe a knit cap pulled low to conceal his fuzzy ears, he could easily fool anyone around. That wouldn't get him farther than the ship's deck, but it would give him access to the boxes.

Sebastian couldn't remember exactly when the fantastic brain finally shut off for the night, but he slept undisturbed until John woke him up by whistling in the shower.

Sebastian ate his breakfast: tuna, chicken, and cheese with egg. It was not as satisfying as a hamburger, but it would keep the terrific body nourished for the job at hand. As soon as he'd finished eating, a blueberry tart popped out of the toaster. Sebastian rounded out his breakfast with that.

John came into the kitchen and stopped to stare at the toaster. "Hmmm, I thought I put a tart in before I showered. I must be getting absentminded. Oh, well, you finished your breakfast, huh, fellow. Sorry, old man, but I'm going to have to leave you home again. I just don't want you mixing with any customs dogs on the docks. They'll be out in full force today, I'm sure."

Sebastian rolled his eyes and whimpered, turning his head to hide the panting grin that spread across his face. Just as he wanted it—no humans to get in his way.

He counted to twenty after he heard the car leave, then pushed through the doggie door and out into the bright sunshine. What a lovely day to catch a smuggler!

He trotted eagerly toward the port. He loped across the high bridge that crossed the channel. A cargo ship, its deck loaded with rail cars, passed under him, heading out to sea. And a fishing trawler, already low in the water from its catch, was coming in. Sea gulls screamed and dove toward its deck, which was strewn with ice chests. Sebastian's nostrils quivered as he inhaled the strong fish smell. Ah, his nose was working perfectly today.

At the docks, he checked a wall map and found that even-numbered berths were on this side of the channel and odd-numbered berths on the other. So far, so good. He slipped into a warehouse and found a pair of overalls hanging on a nail. A knit cap lay on a bench nearby. Quickly he wiggled into them. He spotted a hook stuck in a bale of hay by the door. Snatching that in his teeth, he trotted outside. He discovered he was now at Berth 30, six berths away from where the *Cleopatra* would dock, four away from where the *Bastet* would berth later.

When he reached Berth 38, a ship was preparing for departure. According to the print on its side, it was called *Thutmos I*. It was being loaded with big boxes stamped MEDICAL SUPPLIES. The customs dogs strolled up and down the stacks of boxes, sniffing. They were probably sniffing for illegal exports of weapons to countries that weren't supposed to get them.

Sebastian sniffed, too. He sniffed again. He knew that smell, and it wasn't medicine. It was oil, like the oil that John used to clean his weapon before department inspections.

How could these dogs miss it? At least one of them was trained to sniff out packing grease for weapons. Yet the dogs trotted right by as if they suspected nothing.

He had to let the customs men know. He rose on

his hind legs and threw his body against the box on top. Off it slid. The crate split open. Out spilled medical supplies.

"Hey!" one of the customs inspectors yelled. He pulled back on his dog's leash and ran over to the box.

Sebastian swallowed hard. How could he have been so wrong? Was his nose ruined forever?

The customs man tried to pick up the box. A board fell off, and heavily greased rifles and carbines slid to the concrete floor.

Both customs men scrambled into action, halting the loading and demanding to check everything already on board.

Sebastian felt better about his own nose. But what about those dogs? How could *they* have been so wrong? He touched the first dog's nose with his own. He sniffed. He touched the second dog's nose. The same. Their noses had been rubbed with vanilla extract. That was all they could smell. Just as all he had been able to smell was turpentine.

Maybe later he could figure out a way to let the customs men know what was wrong with their sniffing dogs. But for now he had something else to do. He left the customs men yelling for the loading to stop and calling for backup, and trotted on toward Berth 42, where the *Cleopatra* would be docking soon.

At the warehouse by Berth 42, there was a van parked. It said Karmine Kennels. Karmine—pronounced the same as Carmine? Was it Carmine Rothwinger? Was he just spelling his name differently to make it look better with Kennels? And what would his dogs be doing here?

Sebastian crept closer. He saw John and Hasan. They were talking to a man in a customs uniform. There was also a man in a brown uniform that said KARMINE KENNELS.

John reached down to pet one of the dogs, a German shepherd. "I don't understand, Roger. You use privately owned dogs for your sniffing?" John asked the customs man.

"Oh, no! They are our own handpicked dogs. And we do our own training, too," Roger answered. "But we house them in a privately owned kennel. That way they get all their immunization shots, feed, grooming, and housing cheaper than if we had to maintain our own—"

A dockside phone rang, and the customs man answered. "What? They didn't even sniff it out? You think maybe the dogs are sick or something? I don't know, but the Karmine guy's here right now. I'll try to find out what's going on."

Sebastian realized that Roger was hearing about the dogs at Berth 38. The man in the kennel uniform looked a little pale. He must have realized it, too. "I guess I'd better be going," he told John and Hasan. He trotted toward his van.

"Hold it!" Roger yelled at him. "I want to talk—"

The man broke into a run. "Catch him!" Roger shouted. Sebastian was about to go after him, but fortunately John and Hasan seemed to realize what was happening. John made a running leap and tackled the man, throwing him to the ground. By the time John had scrambled to his feet, Hasan was pulling the man toward the customs officer.

"I didn't do nothing!" the man yelled.

"Then why did you run?" John wanted to know. "If you haven't done anything, we'll know soon enough. And if you have, we'll know that, too. Now, what's all this about?" he asked Roger.

"I don't know what's going on, either," the customs man said, "but I'm sure going to find out. That was our man at Berth 38 I was talking to. He said his dogs didn't detect a load of weapons going out. They wouldn't ever have been discovered if some klutz of a longshoreman hadn't dropped one of the cases."

In his hiding place, Sebastian squared his jaw indignantly. Klutz! Were all humans alike? Did not one give him any credit? They wouldn't talk about him like that to his fuzzy face! He sighed. Yes, they would. They did it all the time.

"Somebody has tampered with those dogs—

maybe these dogs, too—and the only time they're out of our sight is when they're with Karmine Kennels," Roger said. "And judging from this fellow's reaction, I'd say that's where the answer is."

Hasan squatted down with his face near the dogs. He rubbed their ears and talked soothingly to them. Hasan leaned forward and sniffed. He wrinkled his nose. "Vanilla!" he said. "These dogs' noses have been rubbed with vanilla extract. When I was a child and we raised sheep, my father would rub the nose of a ewe with vanilla so she would accept an orphan lamb as her own. She thought that she and it smelled the same. It is an old farming trick."

The customs man shook his head, bewildered. "We'll begin a complete investigation, of course. If you will arrest this man on suspicion, that will keep him from warning whomever he's working for."

While they waited for a squad car with uniformed police to take the man back to the precinct, John read the man his rights. "You have the right to remain silent. You have the right to an attorney. . . . "

At least the man couldn't tell Rothwinger—if it *was* Rothwinger—that the police were on to his little game. But the cagey canine realized there was still work to be done.

"In the meantime, we're going to have to depend on ourselves to find your missing artifacts," the customs man said, echoing Sebastian's thoughts.

Not to worry. He, Sebastian (Super Sleuth), was on the job. And clues were beginning to fall into place. He was sure the business register would show that Karmine Kennels was only one of Carmine Rothwinger's businesses. There was Carmine Ship Lines, too. No wonder he got rich. He was smuggling things in and out and doctoring the dogs so they wouldn't detect anything illegal.

And Sebastian was sure he had another thing figured out, too. The culprit was Rothwinger—it had to be. Carmine Rothwinger had had all those replicas made of Egyptian artifacts. He had invited the public to look at them. People could easily testify that the pieces were fake. But Rothwinger had said that after satisfying the public's curiosity he was going to close his doors forever.

Sebastian was certain that Rothwinger was then going to substitute the real pieces for the fakes. He would be free to display and enjoy them without anyone ever being the least bit suspicious. Rothwinger was one of those eccentrics Hasan mentioned. But he had an extra helping of cunning!

His plan might have worked, too, had it not been for this detective. But Sebastian was getting ahead of himself, wasn't he? He still had to prove his theory. And he still had to find the stolen artifacts. A tad more difficult than theorizing, even for the four-on-the-floor furry detective.

7
All That Ends Well

By the time the patrol car had picked up the kennel man, the *Cleopatra* had arrived in port. Stealthily, Sebastian watched John and Hasan, armed with their warrant, board the *Cleopatra* for a search, as they had done with each docking ship. Slipping aboard in the confusion that followed, he observed the two of them upturning bunk mattresses, opening luggage, and thumping cabinets for hollow cavities that might secret the artifacts away.

For hours, they prodded, pushed, and pulled everything on the ship. They opened every box of dates; all they found were dates. They peered into every crate of olives; all they found were olives. And they thumped every barrel of olive oil to see if it thudded instead of sloshed. Nothing.

"They just aren't here," John said, obviously exasperated. "Let's hope we have more luck with the *Bastet*. It should be docked by now."

The three of them—John and Hasan in the open

and Sebastian skulking in the shadows of warehouses—went to Berth 38, where the *Bastet* now stood, its boarding plank still up and customs officers lining the dock to be sure that no one left the ship.

John and Hasan went aboard and presented their search warrant to the captain, who shouted at them in a foreign language. Sebastian didn't understand, but he didn't need a translation to tell that the man was angry.

On board, they went through the same routine. They checked above and below decks. They even looked inside the smokestacks. Again, nothing.

How could he have been so wrong? Sebastian wondered.

"How could we have been so wrong?" John asked Hasan. "I felt sure we were on to something, especially after we found the dogs had been messed up for sniffing."

"I don't understand it, either, my friend John. I was positive that this Rothwinger was our man. Alas, nothing. I don't know what to do, except continue to search ships. I fear, though, we are too late."

Sebastian shed the overalls and cap and sat down on the dock's edge to think. He scratched a flea behind his left ear and watched idly as the fishing trawlers wove their way down the channel to their own docks.

Sea gulls dove and screamed at the trawlers, begging for a taste of their catch. And on board, the fishermen worked to sort their catches into the ice chests, ready for sale. Amusing how the little boats were all named, just as the big ships were.

I Sea U, The Betsy Lou, Nefertiti, N Debt—all of them paraded past. The men seemed to pay no attention at all to those noisy, pushy, diving birds.

Except for the *Nefertiti*, the birds were giving those boats a hard time. Wait a minute. Why weren't the birds diving at that boat? Its ice chests lined its deck, just as ice chests lined the other trawlers. Didn't they catch anything? *Nefertiti*—if memory served him right (and it always did)—was the name of an Egyptian queen. Egyptian! Of course, Carmine just couldn't resist, could he?

Sebastian made a dash for John—he had to get his attention. He yanked on John's pant leg, rumbling deep in his throat.

"Wha—" John nearly lost his balance. "Sebastian! You followed me, you naughty—"

Sebastian didn't wait. He ran along the dock, keeping pace with the *Nefertiti*. He could hear John behind him, yelling, "Come back, boy. Come, Sebastian." And he could hear Hasan right behind John, yelling, "What is it? What is going on?"

They'd find out soon enough, if they kept up with the old hairy hawkshaw. The trawler eased alongside a small pier, and the captain shut its motor down to a slow thrumming. Sebastian took a deep breath and made a dog's-width leap, landing with a thud on deck. A faint scent of gunpowder teased his nose. Was it from Hasan's spent bullets?

A man with a ship tattooed on his arm and holding a burlap bag tied at the top started yelling. Sebastian was sure the bag had at least a couple of the stolen artifacts in it. He bit into the bag and tugged. The man tugged back, kicking at Sebastian.

John jumped on board. Help at last! "Here, now," John yelled at him. "Let go of that bag, you naughty dog. I'm so sorry!"

Sebastian yanked back, growling, and the bag flew open, spilling dirty laundry all over the deck of the boat.

Startled, Sebastian let go. John tugged at his neck fur. "When I get you home, it's dry dog food for a week!" he scolded. "I'm so sorry," John told the man with the tattoo. "I just don't know what has come over him. I hope he didn't hurt anything."

The man snarled and gathered the clothes back into the bag. "Just get 'im away from here."

Subdued and embarrassed, Sebastian followed John onto the dock. He had been so sure this time. What about the sea gulls? They didn't seem to think the boat had any fish on board. Surely if they'd smelled fish, they'd have been diving at the boat.

And he'd been so sure he'd smelled gunpowder from spent bullets.

He plodded along the dock, sulking as John told him all the things that he wasn't going to get to do after this. He gave one last unhappy glance at the *Nefertiti*. The tattooed man and the one who'd been driving the boat were carrying an ice chest onto a truck that had backed up to the dock.

Wait a minute. *Both* of them carrying one ice chest? Hadn't the man yesterday carried one all by himself? And neither of these men looked like a weakling. There was only one thing that could make that chest as heavy as it seemed to be. And those ice chests were just big enough to hold bread boxes. They'd be perfect for hiding the artifacts. With one mighty jerk Sebastian freed himself from John's grasp. He dashed toward the *Nefertiti* with John and Hasan only footsteps behind. John was really angry this time. Sebastian had better be right!

With a great leap, Sebastian jumped against the tattooed man's shoulders. The man lost his balance, and both of them tumbled head first into the water.

Dog-paddling, Sebastian managed to propel himself to the dock, where Hasan pulled him out of the water. He shook vigorously, sending a rain of water over John, the boat pilot, and the open ice chest.

Sebastian pushed the chest onto its side. A box inside had broken open, and packing material spilled

out. A shiny brass bullet rolled from the packing and clattered onto the dock. There, looking back, was the golden head of a lion with turquoise inlays.

Hasan fished the tattooed man out of the water and handcuffed him. By that time John had handcuffed the other man. "You are both under arrest," John told them. "You have the right to remain silent. You . . ."

They stepped aboard the trawler and found the rest of the small artifacts in the other ice chests. The larger pieces were in the hold below decks.

John called for a patrol car to take the captain and the tattooed sailor to jail, where they just couldn't wait to tell the police that it was Carmine Rothwinger who had hired them to bring in the stolen artifacts. Rothwinger had known that the police would probably be watching the ships. So he'd sent out one of his fishing trawlers, the *Nefertiti*, to lay alongside the *Bastet* and take on the artifacts, which they then put into the ice chests.

Of course, Rothwinger hadn't counted on someone as clever as Sebastian. Just as the old crime hound had thought, Rothwinger had planned on substituting the real artifacts for his phony ones. He could have displayed them smugly, and after all the publicity about his phony ones, no one would have suspected the switch.

There were so many ways this case might have

gone awry. The thieves might have repacked the artifacts, discarding the spent bullets. And even if the artifacts had remained in their telltale cases (as they had), the dogs might have been tampered with (as they had been to allow an export out). Or the old super sleuth himself might have concentrated on the incoming ships, ignoring the small commercial and private boats that frequented the channel. Or the captain of the *Nefertiti* might have decided to go fishing while he was waiting for the contraband. In that case, his boat would have been just as fishy as the others, and the clever canine might never have noticed. There was an awful lot of luck involved in solving mysteries, Sebastian thought. Luck coupled with clever detection, that is.

Catching Rothwinger ended all his dirty dealings, smuggling arms out of the country, smuggling stolen goods in, and tampering with the customs dogs.

When Rothwinger and his helpers had been booked and jailed and photographs of the artifacts on the boat had been made for evidence, Hasan, with the help of the city museum, packed the precious treasures for their return. The boxes had first-class airline tickets—no cargo hold for them.

"I will miss you, my friend John—and my new friend, Sebastian," Hasan said before boarding. He scratched Sebastian's ear. *Mmmm.*

"Two days is much too short a visit, Hasan," John

said. "But I'm glad this case ended well. If it hadn't been for that klutzy longshoreman uncovering that box of weapons, and if Sebastian hadn't been so naughty and followed me, then jumped on that man and fallen overboard . . . "

"Ah, yes," Hasan said. "Such a lucky accident." He winked at Sebastian, chuckling.

Sebastian couldn't be sure, but he thought perhaps Hasan did understand. It was nice to think so, anyway.

He offered his paw to Hasan, who shook it quickly, then hurried to board his plane. He sniffed the air, testing the old nose. There was bubble gum nearby, raspberry flavor. And tobacco, a diet soda, and mustard. Mustard? If there was mustard, there must be a hamburger or a hot dog.

His nose led him to a gentleman who'd fallen asleep, probably waiting for his plane. The hot dog tilted dangerously near his tie.

Sebastian leaned close and slurped the hot dog down in one big gulp. It was the kind thing to do. Should he have let the man's tie get ruined?

"Sebastian!" John shouted. "Ready, boy?"

What kind of question was that? A super sleuth, especially a four-on-the-floor variety, was *always* ready for *anything.*

Other books about Sebastian

Mary Blount Christian

SEBASTIAN
[Super Sleuth]
and the
Mystery Patient

Illustrated by Lisa McCue

Macmillan Publishing Company   New York

Collier Macmillan Canada   Toronto

Maxwell Macmillan International Publishing Group
New York   Oxford   Singapore   Sydney

Remembering Jimmie Dill Lee.
Her courage and determination
live on through inspiration.

Text copyright © 1991 by Mary Blount Christian
Illustrations copyright © 1991 by Lisa McCue
All rights reserved. No part of this book may be reproduced
or transmitted in any form or by any means, electronic
or mechanical, including photocopying, recording, or by any
information storage and retrieval system,
without permission in writing from the Publisher.
Macmillan Publishing Company
866 Third Avenue
New York, NY 10022
Collier Macmillan Canada, Inc.
1200 Eglinton Avenue East
Suite 200
Don Mills, Ontario M3C 3N1
First edition
Printed in the United States of America

10 9 8 7 6 5 4 3 2 1

The text of this book is set in 12 point Primer.
The illustrations are rendered in scratchboard.
Library of Congress Cataloging-in-Publication Data
Christian, Mary Blount.
Sebastian Super Sleuth and the mystery patient / Mary Blount
Christian : illustrated by Lisa McCue.
p.   cm.
Summary: Dog detective Sebastian helps his master protect a
mystery patient at City Hospital at a time when an attempted coup
has just occurred in a nation friendly to the United States.
ISBN 0-02-718571-0
[1. Dogs—Fiction. 2. Mystery and detective stories.] I. McCue.
Lisa, ill. II. Title.
PZ7.C4528Sei 1991 [Fic]—dc20   90-45092

Contents

1
How's a Dog to Know?

Sebastian sprang from his sleeping spot on the couch, his radar ears rotating, keen eyes searching, and nose quivering. He was the very picture of a canine detective ready for anything. What was that growling noise?

Arrrrrrrrg. Glaaaaaaaaaa.

Had another dog slipped through the doggie door that was left open for his midnight ramblings? Although it seemed impossible that anything could get past Sebastian's ever-ready alertness, something was making a terrible, threatening noise, which was coming from the direction of John's bedroom.

John! Was his human in danger? John Quincy Jones, a detective with the City Police Department, should be able to take care of himself. However, it was Sebastian (Super Sleuth), John's unpaid partner, who usually wound up taking care of John, especially when it came to solving cases. And now his friend and partner in crime-solving was in danger.

Sebastian leaped from the couch and raced into the bedroom, muscles tensed for whatever danger might be waiting. He had his own canine kung-fu tactics, which he would not hesitate to use in defense of his human.

Arrrrrrrrg. Glaaaaaaaaaa.

The sound was coming from the bathroom. Cautiously, Sebastian nosed the door open and peered inside. John was alone at the sink with his head thrown back, making those awful noises.

Arrrrrrrrg. Glaaaaaaaaaa.

John spat into the sink and ran water. He glanced over at Sebastian with slightly glazed eyes. "Oh, good morning, fellow. Did I wake you up with my gargling? My throat is sore, and my tonsils are swollen. I can barely swallow."

He swallowed and moaned. "Maybe I'd better take the day off. I hardly feel like tracking criminals." He touched his forehead. "I feel feverish. I can't eat a thing this morning."

It distressed the old hairy hawkshaw to see his human under the weather and not eating. But *his* throat was fine, and he felt like eating a lot. Maybe he'd eat a little extra this morning, for John.

"Well, I guess my sore throat doesn't affect *your* appetite, huh, fellow?" John said, strolling into the kitchen. Sebastian trailed close behind, the stub of his tail wiggling as he anticipated breaking his fast of the night. Of the last few hours, anyway, since he'd had that bit of leftover pizza their neighbor had thrown away. How could anyone throw away a perfectly good piece of pizza?

Sebastian sat by his bowl as John rummaged through the cabinet, pulling out a can with a picture of a dog on it. The can opener whirred, and a waft of sweet smells filled the room.

John put a piece of newspaper on the floor, then set the bowl on top and spooned the meat into it. Sebastian couldn't imagine why John tried to protect the floor from spilled food. Had he, Sebastian (Super Sleuth), ever left so much as a crumb of anything edible within reach of his tongue? He did appreciate the newspaper, however. It gave him the chance to catch up on world news as he ate. He gave his human a grateful lick on the face. John's nose was dry and hot, not moist and cool like his own. John really was sick. Maybe he should see the veterinarian.

When John had left, Sebastian ate and scanned the news. The local football team had sunk to last place. The symphony orchestra had left on a European tour. The president said there was no truth to the rumors that he wouldn't run for another term, and the country of Balmunio had put down another coup attempt by a renegade general.

Gingerly, Sebastian slurped up a bit of food that had fallen over the story. He then read that President Eduardo Mardatia was safely inside his presidential palace, surrounded by friendly guards, and would appear live on television later today to quash supporters' fears that he was no longer running his country.

Sebastian fervently hoped that President Mardatia would be all right. The United States needed a friendly government in that part of the world, and the renegade general was a sworn enemy of ours.

The still-hungry canine wolfed down the meager meal, chasing his scooting bowl across the floor to get the very last morsel. He licked his lips, partially satisfied. That had been nice. But was it *all*?

John was back in the bathroom, rummaging through the medicine cabinet for some throat lozenges. He popped one into his mouth and sighed mournfully. "No work today, big fellow. I'm just going to lie down awhile and melt this lozenge. Then I'll call Chief and tell—"

The phone rang as John flopped back on the bed, closing his eyes. After the second ring, the answering machine clicked on and Chief's raucous roar drifted through the apartment.

"John! I know you're there and hear this, so don't pretend otherwise. Get your lazy bones into my office right now. On the double! You hear? John? John!"

Moaning, John picked up the extension. "Chief, I was just about to call you. I'm feeling terrible this morning. My throat, you know. I thought maybe I'd take the day off and rest, have some soup and fruit juices and—"

Sebastian made a face. Now that John had picked up the extension, he could hear only John's side of the conversation. Why didn't John punch the speaker button? It was so rude to act as if Sebastian weren't there and interested.

"Uh huh. Uh huh. Yessir. Yessir. I understand. I'm on my way, Chief." John hung up the phone. "Phooey!" he said. "I have to go to work, after all."

I? How could John forget his hairy and capable canine partner?

A little later, they arrived at the door marked Chief of Police. John tapped on the door, then opened it and peeked inside. "It's me, Chief. May I come in?"

I again. What was the matter? Was he invisible, or something?

"Get in here, Detective Jones. Now!"

John scooted in, and Sebastian trotted in behind him.

"That fleabag isn't shedding, is he? I don't want fur all over my carpet," Chief said.

Sebastian showed his disapproval of Chief's insults by pointing his nose into the air. He sniffed indignantly. His nose quivered as it recognized a familiar scent. He sniffed again, picking up the smell of a croissant stuffed with—um, yes, that was it—stuffed with ham and cheese. He could always count on Chief to have some delicious delicacy stashed in his office.

With one ear cocked to the conversation, Sebas-

5

tian strolled casually around the office, looking for the source of the delicious smell. Chief had a habit of hiding his food from Sebastian. He didn't like to share. Sebastian felt it was his responsibility to coax Chief into better manners. It was their little game. Chief hid the food. Sebastian found and devoured it. Except Chief didn't like to play.

There it was, on Chief's desk under a pile of papers. Sebastian edged closer.

"I want you to go to City Hospital and check out the security. We'll need to stop public access to certain areas. See how we can secure a floor and a room on that floor, even if we have to close down the whole floor and have a uniform accompanying all medical personnel into the room. Got it? Stairwells, elevators, halls, everything."

"Got it! What's up, Chief? Why all that security? Some rock-'n'-roll star going into the hospital?" John winced as he swallowed, then popped another lozenge into his mouth.

"*Somebody* is going into the hospital—today. The rest you'll know when you need to know, and not until then, understand?" Chief glared at Sebastian.

Sebastian's ears perked up as he edged toward the croissant, his nose quivering. What did Chief mean, when they needed to know? They were police, weren't they?

"But, Chief!" John protested, echoing Sebastian's thoughts. "Why can't I know whom I'm protecting?"

Chief leaned back in his chair. "Let's just say it's a matter of national security. And the more people who know, the more likely it is that the secret will get out. And that's dangerous." Chief cleared his throat importantly. "Of course, *I* know."

Wow! It had to be something really big to keep it a secret from even them.

"But—"

Scowling, Chief said, "Listen, do you think that if I had anybody else I'd be sending you? It's just that half my detectives are out sick today with some virus or flu or something. I'm desperate."

John sighed. "Thanks for your confidence, Chief. But I don't feel well myself. I have this sore—"

"Forget it, John!" Chief growled. "Just investigate security there and see that nothing and no one can get in or out without *our* wanting it."

John pushed himself feebly from the chair. "Right, Chief."

"And, John," Chief said. "Ditch the mutt. No dogs allowed at the hospital, you know."

Sebastian's mouth flew open in shock. Not allowed? But he was needed! Surely the hospital could make an exception for a doggie detective. After all, the animal clinic let humans in. Distraught, Sebastian snapped up the croissant, downing it in two easy swallows.

7

Chief's fist slammed the desk dangerously near Sebastian's nose. "On second thought, ditch the mutt permanently!" He shoved Sebastian. "Get out of here, you four-legged garbage disposal."

Sebastian trotted through the door John had just opened, nose in the air. *Humpt!* Hurl insults at him, would he? Bar him from a case, would he?

Chief would be sorry! Sebastian vowed to himself.

2
If Walls Could Talk

In the hospital parking lot, Sebastian jammed his head outside the car window and stared up at the tall building that was City Hospital. An orange wind sock on the roof stood straight out, indicating that the wind was coming from the east. If the wind sock was on the roof, the helicopters used for air ambulances must land up there when they brought patients to the hospital. Patients probably entered the hospital through an elevator that went up to the roof.

With its many windows, some whited out by closed drapes and others darker where the drapes were open, the building looked almost like a checkerboard. What secret did this building hold? If only walls could talk.

"I'm sorry, old fellow," John said, patting Sebastian on the head. "But you'll have to stay in the car. It's cool, though, and I'll leave the windows down so you'll have plenty of air. But you must stay. You understand? Stay!"

Sebastian rolled his eyes pitifully and whimpered. That was always good for some immediate sympathy and a later apology in the form of food.

He touched John's warm nose with his own cool one. If John took that as a yes, so be it. It was only meant as a comforting gesture.

Sebastian's gaze followed John as he wove his way through the white-clad people strolling in and out of the building. Sebastian waited until John was safely inside, then leaped through the window and trotted toward the building.

No dogs allowed, indeed! Who did they think they were, keeping out the most valuable half of a detective team just because he was fuzzier than the other partner and walked on four legs?

It had to be an error. However, there was a big sign at the entrance. NO DOGS ALLOWED, EXCEPT SEEING EYE. NO CHILDREN UNDER TWELVE. Discrimination at its worst!

He sat on his haunches and looked toward the wind sock. Maybe he could go up the fire escape and enter through the helipad door on the roof. He shivered slightly. No, he'd do that as a very last resort. Heights were his enemy, one of the few that frightened him.

Trotting around to the side of the building, he spotted an emergency entrance and parking spaces for loading and unloading ambulances. He watched as two men in white coats rolled a patient on a gurney, a stretcher on wheels. As they neared the entrance, doors swung open, probably automatically. They took the gurney inside.

There was a second gurney, empty except for a pile of rumpled sheets, near the entrance. Sebastian scooted over and leaped onto the gurney, wiggling until he was sure the sheets covered him completely.

"Hey, Sam," someone near him shouted. "What's this patient doing outside? Get this gurney into emergency ASAP, as soon as possible. I oughtta put you on report!"

Sebastian felt himself being wheeled along. He was sure he was inside, because there were sounds of bustling feet and chatter. "Get Doc Randall and let's get some vital statistics on this patient. Stat!" a gruff voice yelled. Sebastian had heard that word on TV shows. Stat was what medical people yelled when they wanted others to hurry.

As the squishy sounds of crepe-soled shoes faded, Sebastian peeked from under the sheet. He was alone, and a curtain had been pulled around the gurney. He was in a little examining room. Ugh. There were all sorts of instruments of torture in the room.

Quickly, he jumped from the gurney and peeked around the curtain. Everyone seemed busy and distracted. Now was his chance. He skulked through the door and along the walls toward the hallway that was labeled TO LOBBY.

None of the staff took notice. Only a small child looking over a woman's shoulder saw him. "Gog-

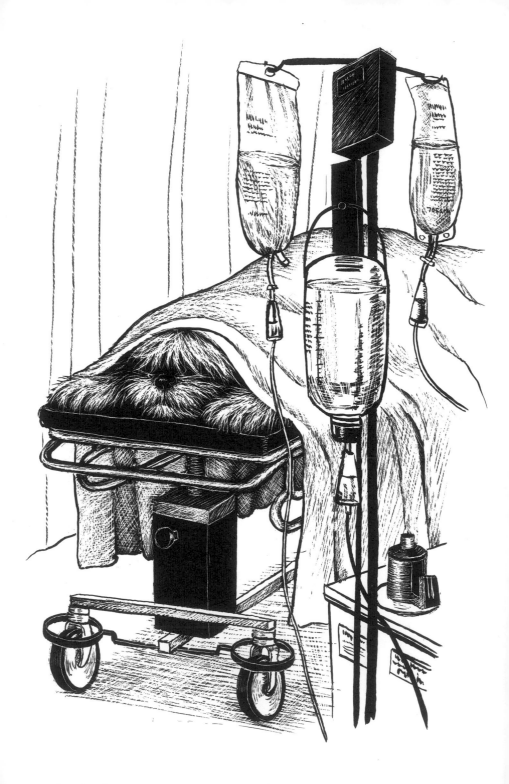

gie! Goggie!" the child yelled, giggling. The woman shushed the child, and Sebastian breathed a sigh of relief.

John was talking with a woman dressed in a long white coat, a stethoscope hanging from her neck. They were standing near an elevator marked STAFF ONLY.

When the doors to the elevator had swooshed shut behind them, Sebastian trotted over and watched the pinpoint light that indicated which floor the elevator was on. It stopped on seven.

Okay, so John and the woman had gotten off on the seventh floor. Sebastian rose on his hind legs and nudged the up button. Keeping an eye out for people who might spot him, he fidgeted nervously until the elevator doors opened with a light ping. Quickly he stepped into the empty elevator and held his breath until the doors shut, leaving him alone and undetected. So far.

Up on his hind legs again, he touched his nose to the express button, then to seven, ensuring that he would not be surprised by unwelcome riders who might get on at other floors.

The elevator whooshed dizzily up to the seventh floor and the doors opened. Cautiously, Sebastian skittered out and crouched behind a cart filled with magazines and snacks. As he considered his next move, he snapped up a package of cheese and crackers and ate them quickly.

Sebastian realized he needed a disguise. Glancing around, he saw a door with a sign: SUPPLIES/ STAFF ONLY. Fortunately, the door was slightly ajar and a gentle push with his nose swung it open wide enough for him to slip inside.

There were gowns for patients—terrible things with open backs—and bed linens, and clothing for hospital personnel. Sebastian sat on his haunches and scratched his ear, thinking. There were many disguises available, but he had to be careful what he chose.

If he was mistaken for a doctor, he might be called upon to make a diagnosis or to do brain surgery. Despite his considerable knowledge, he was not versed in the area of medicine.

A housekeeper's uniform? That would mean pushing a mop around, dusting, and using that stinky liquid cleanser that smelled like a sweaty pine tree. Ah! There, a red-and-white striped pinafore and white blouse. Wasn't that a candy striper's uniform? As a candy striper, a volunteer, he could roam the halls with magazines, juices, and snacks and wouldn't have to do anything medical. And if he got hungry—and didn't he always get hungry while working a case?—there'd be food available. It was perfect!

Sebastian wiggled into the candy striper's blouse and pinafore. The little hat with the starched cotton veil attached at the back was a bit more difficult to maneuver into, but it was part of the uniform. If candy stripers wore one, *he'd* have to, also.

The cart Sebastian had been hiding behind earlier must belong to the candy striper. Slipping into the hall, he rose on his hind legs, placed his paws on the cart, and pushed. It rolled easily. Not bad. With his paws resting on the cart, it was easy to walk on his hind legs.

John and the woman were at the other end of the hall, so Sebastian pushed the cart toward them. Maybe he could eavesdrop and find out what this case was all about.

"It would make security so much easier if we could lock the doors leading to the stairwells," John told the woman.

She shook her head vigorously. "To comply with fire regulations, we have to leave the doors to the stairwells unlocked. Besides, our personnel often use the stairs. The elevators can be terribly slow, and every moment counts."

"I understand that, Dr. Payne. It was only wishful thinking," John said.

Dr. Payne frowned at John and placed her fingers against his neck on both sides. "Your face is flushed with fever, and the glands in your neck are swollen considerably. Has your doctor looked at you?"

John threw his hand up protectively. "I—I don't

have a regular doctor. Except for this sore throat, I'm the picture of good health."

The doctor smiled. "So I can see. Come to the nurses' station, and I'll take a look at your throat. Humor me, why don't you? Even if you feel marvelous."

Drawing back, John shook his head. "I don't have time to be sick. I need to finish this security check." He swallowed, and from John's expression Sebastian could tell it was painful.

The doctor turned toward the candy striper's cart and grabbed a can of apple juice. "Then at least drink this," she told John, handing him the pop-top can. "The liquid will soothe your throat a little."

John and the doctor strolled up and down the wide hall, with Sebastian pushing the cart just behind them, listening.

John poked his head into one patient room after another. "This room, seven-seventy-seven, would be the best one for your mystery patient," he said. "It's not connected to any other room through a common bathroom, and it's in full view of the nurses' station. A guard posted in front of its door would see all the stairwells and elevators. No one could get past him." John rubbed his throat, wincing. "Yet I'd feel better if we had a buffer of empty rooms above, below, and on each side of it."

"I'll do what I can," Dr. Payne promised. "But we are, after all, a hospital. If those rooms are needed, they must be occupied. Are you expecting someone to drill through a wall, ceiling, or floor to get to my patient? Be reasonable!"

John scowled at her. "Doctor, we are all going to do what we have to do to protect this mystery patient, even if it means diverting other patients to other hospitals."

Dr. Payne stiffened, but said, "Yes, of course. I understand, but you'll need to clear that with hospital administrators and inform admitting."

Nodding approvingly, John said, "We'll need to have someone in the operating room and the recovery room, too."

"No way!" Dr. Payne said. "I absolutely forbid it. My patient is *my* responsibility in OR and recovery. *Your* job begins when he gets out here. I want only my staff with me at such an important time. The operating rooms have no space for extra personnel. The guards might get in the way at a critical moment. I can't risk that."

John narrowed his eyes at Dr. Payne, as if studying her. "Can you trust every member of your staff? How can we guarantee that there'll be no trouble in the operating room?"

Crossing her arms and raising her chin to a defiant level, Dr. Payne hissed her words through narrowed lips. "My OR staff has been with me for years. They are completely loyal to me and to their country, I can assure you. We'll close the observa-

17

tion room during the procedure, and we'll allow no one but the special nurses we've known for many years in the recovery room, where we'll hold the patient until he rouses from the anesthesia."

Dr. Payne continued. "You can have someone at his bedside in the intensive care unit. Because it is a more open area, with patients' relatives coming in and out, we will keep him in ICU only until his vital signs look good. We will set up the private room with all the machinery he'll need and move him there as soon as it is safe, which should be after several hours.

"The operation takes around four hours. He'll be in the recovery room for several more, then in the intensive care unit while we prepare his private room. That means you won't have to worry about him until at least seven hours after he is first admitted," she said. "And only when he is in room seven-seventy-seven—*your* area of responsibility."

"What about the staff on this floor? Have you hired anyone since you knew you would be operating on the mystery patient?" John wanted to know.

"No one," she replied. "We have some new faces on seven, but they are not new to the hospital. They've been brought up from other floors to substitute for sick employees. While they have worked different floors and different shifts and probably won't know one another, they are all longtime employees of the hospital, and they've all been checked out, as even I have, by the FBI. No one will be brought in from outside this hospital. You and your people are welcome to go through the personnel files, too, although it seems unnecessary to me."

John bristled. "We'll have to decide what is necessary, Dr. Payne. And I'm sure my chief is in full cooperation with the FBI and the CIA and anyone else needed to protect Mr. Mystery. Or is it Ms. Mystery?"

Dr. Payne shrugged. "It is Mr. Mystery. But even I don't know my patient, except by X rays and blood type and the fact that he'll be undergoing a quadruple bypass. The fewer people who know his identity, the better, according to the State Depart—" Her eyes widened.

John's eyebrows rose slightly. "State Department? Then he is not a U.S. citizen?"

Sebastian licked his whiskers, thinking. A matter of national security. Not a U.S. citizen. A man. Who could this be?

"Forget I said that," Dr. Payne warned. "I misspoke."

John smiled at her, nodding. "Certainly. Well, we will have an armed uniform at the door at all times. That alone is usually enough to discourage intruders. We'll also have undercover protection. So don't be surprised to see a new housekeeper or janitor or two." John swallowed hard, visibly

19

cringing. "Besides, if we don't know much about the mystery patient, how can anyone else know?"

Sebastian scowled. There were plenty of national secrets known to everyone, including foreign governments. Didn't a toy company come out with a plastic model of a military plane that was supposed to be such a big secret? It hit the market months before the public got the first look at the real one. What if the good guys were the only ones who didn't know about this secret?

John was not the best of help when he was healthy. And he was not feeling even close to good today.

Someone was in terrible danger, and the old sleuth hound didn't even know whom he was to protect. That made his job difficult. But no job was impossible for such a clever canine as he!

3
When All Else Fails . . .

Sebastian hovered near the nurses' station while John phoned in his report and suggestions to Chief. When he'd hung up, John turned to Dr. Payne and said, "The wheels are already in motion. We'll have this place tight and secure within a few hours, ready for your mystery patient whenever he arrives."

John strolled toward the elevator with Dr. Payne, and Sebastian followed closely behind them.

"I'll be relieved when this man has recuperated and gone," Dr. Payne said. "It seems weird that we've made heart surgery relatively safe and almost routine, yet my patient could still be in grave danger."

John cleared his throat. "You take care of the heart, Dr. Payne. We'll take care of the security. As soon as—" John's eyelids fluttered, then closed. His face went pale.

Sebastian's heart thumped in his chest and his breath caught in his throat as his human crumpled into a heap on the hospital floor.

"Get a gurney, stat!" Dr. Payne yelled. Orderlies and nurses and nurses' aides scattered in every di-

rection. A nurse brought smelling salts, and Dr. Payne broke open the package and held the saturated cotton wad under John's nose. Almost immediately he blinked, then opened his eyes, looking glazed and confused.

"Lie still," Dr. Payne commanded as a second nurse brought a blood pressure monitor, wrapped the band around John's arm, and pumped air into the band.

"BP is one-thirty-nine over eighty-five," she told Dr. Payne as the band gradually deflated and the attached clocklike device registered John's blood pressure. His blood pressure was not dangerously high, but it was higher than usual, Sebastian noted. It did show that his body was under stress. Someone else jammed a thermometer into John's mouth. When the thermometer beeped, the nurse checked it. "It's a hundred and two, doctor."

His poor human! John had a high temperature. He really was sick!

Two orderlies scooped John up and placed him on a gurney. Sebastian fought the urge to rush to John's side, to lick his face and assure him that he was going to be all right. If he was caught, he'd be even less help to his human than he was now.

Sebastian hovered near the gurney as Dr. Payne moved her stethoscope over John's chest, listening. "Your heartbeat is within the normal range. Your problem is obviously those tonsils," Dr. Payne said.

"You should've seen a physician right away, instead of coming to work today." She turned to a nurse and instructed her to begin an IV.

Sebastian shuddered with the memory of needles. He wanted to help John escape, yet he remembered what John always told him. "It's for your own good, fellow. And the pain will be no worse than a flea bite." Well, that was bad enough.

John said raspingly, "But the case! The mystery patient—"

"You won't do my patient much good if you collapse again. You really need to have those tonsils out as soon as your fever breaks, or they'll give you more trouble," Dr. Payne said. "I'm a heart surgeon, but I can turn you over to Dr. Ryan, since you don't have your own doctor. He's three floors down, where they do the general surgery."

John moaned. "I don't have time to be sick. I don't have time for surgery. I don't want to be here."

Dr. Payne smiled at him and patted his shoulder. "Nobody does. But a tonsillectomy is a simple procedure. You'll be home in a couple of days and up almost immediately, barring complications."

Complications? What sort of complications? Sebastian shook uncontrollably.

"Complications? What sort of complications?" John asked. He struggled to get up.

Dr. Payne pushed him back gently. "Nothing!

Really! You're going to be fine; you seem otherwise healthy. The nurse will take you down to the fourth floor. They have a room waiting for you, and Dr. Ryan will be there. Is there someone I should notify for you?"

"Oh, my gosh!" John said. "Chief! And my fiancée, Maude Culpepper. Oh, no! My dog! My poor dog is in a car downstairs. If you can call Maude at her work she'll come down and get Sebastian."

It was sweet of John to think of him during John's hour of pain, but Sebastian could take care of himself. And he didn't want Maude or that silly Lady Sharon interfering with his investigation.

"Give me your fiancée's number, and I'll call her. You can report to your chief on the phone in your room," Dr. Payne said.

Now that his human was under the care of the hospital, the four-on-the-floor hawkshaw had a case to solve. Besides, he didn't want to be too far away from John. He would surely feel—well, lonely—without his human.

He watched John's gurney disappear into the elevator, then watched the floor indicator drop to four. He would look in on John later, once he was settled.

Sebastian glanced at the wall clock. After Maude had been notified, it would take her about a half hour to get to the hospital parking lot. He would make it a point to be there in the car, waiting for her. He didn't want her to have any reason to worry John, not now.

"Dr. Payne!" a nurse called breathlessly. "Some man just called. He said your patient John Doe's condition has worsened. They have a chopper standing by at International Airport. They'll fly him here the moment his jet arrives." She glanced at her watch. "Which should be in about fifteen minutes." She looked puzzled. "John Doe? Don't we have a *real* name on this guy?"

"Get OR prepared and have my staff standing by and ready with plenty of O negative blood." Dr. Payne was barking orders with precision quickness. "Get those X rays and charts into OR. Have an elevator at roof level for immediate access. And call the police chief to get some uniforms here ASAP. At this very moment, Detective Jones is probably informing him as to what security steps must be taken. I'll scrub immediately. Stat!"

She pushed a red button on the wall, and double doors marked SURGICAL STAFF ONLY opened suddenly. Dr. Payne disappeared through the doorway.

Sebastian's keen mind switched into double time. If he put on the green scrubs and a surgical mask, he could probably get inside. But, no. Maybe he should go see about John. No, maybe— He felt as if he were chasing his own tail. Sebastian had never been so confused in his life!

He took a couple of deep breaths to calm himself. First things first. Once he knew the mystery patient's identity, he'd have a better idea just who might want him dead. And once he knew that, he'd know better how to protect the man.

He wouldn't let John down. And he wouldn't let his country down.

4

More Questions Than Answers

There was only one nurse at the station. She had just told Chief the news about the mystery patient and hung up the phone. He had to distract her so that he could get into the station and do some detective work.

Slipping into one of the unoccupied patient rooms, he nudged the call button, then scrambled through the connecting bathroom and out the other room.

He watched as the nurse checked the patient call-board. She looked through her charts, obviously puzzled. "I didn't know we had a patient in room seven-seventy," she mumbled. "There's no chart here, either." She hurried down the hall toward 770, and Sebastian scooted behind the desk. He pawed at charts and papers on the desk. There was nothing there about a patient being called John Doe.

He heard the squish-squish of crepe-soled shoes returning, and the nurse muttering about a possible electrical short on the call-board. Quickly he scrambled from behind the desk and returned to the cart. He pushed the cart toward a stairwell and left it at the entrance. As much as he hated walking seven flights of stairs, he wasn't interested in taking a chance on the elevator again.

No sooner had Sebastian shed the candy striper's costume in the stairwell and raced to the car than Maude's car appeared at the entrance to the parking lot. Sebastian rested his chin on the windowsill and gazed soulfully toward the entrance to the hospital. He steadied his breathing so she wouldn't know he'd been running.

Maude jumped from her car, leaving the door open, and rushed to tousle Sebastian's fur, murmuring sympathetic nothings. "You're surprised to see me, aren't you, Sebastian? Well, you won't understand this, of course, but you can't see John for a few days."

Who wouldn't understand? Did she think he was an ordinary dog, or something? Furthermore, try and stop him from seeing his poor sick human!

"Come with me, fellow, and we'll go to visit your friend, Lady Sharon. Now, won't that be fun?"

Fun? Friend? Was she joking?

Maude grabbed Sebastian's collar and guided him into her car, then returned to John's car to roll up the windows and lock it. "I'll get you settled, then come back and stay with John," she said

when she was back in her own car with Sebastian at her side. "Poor darling. I wish he didn't have to have his tonsils out, but he'll feel much better. And he'll be on an ice-cream and Jell-O diet until his stitches heal."

Ice cream? Jell-O? Did dogs have tonsils?

When they reached Maude's house, Lady Sharon yipped and leaped about, licking Sebastian's face in greeting. Sebastian gave a low, rumbling growl. Then Lady Sharon ran to get her squeaky toy. What was a grown dog doing with a rubber mouse?

"That's good," Maude said. "You two play nice, and I'll go see about John. Now, don't you worry, Sebastian. He'll be just fine."

Sebastian ran to the window and watched Maude drive away. When she was out of sight, he trotted into the kitchen and finished the food that Lady Sharon had carelessly left. He'd never understand her reluctance to finish those last delightful nibbles of dog food.

That accomplished, he ran back to the window and pawed at the screen, whimpering. The hook latch moved a little. He jiggled it some more. Finally the hook slid away and the screen hung loose. Now he could easily escape whenever he wanted to.

But he would bide his time. John would have Maude and the hospital staff buzzing about him for hours, so it would be impossible to see him without being detected. By now, the mystery patient should be in surgery. Quadruple bypass, Dr. Payne had said. That would take up to four hours in the operating room. Then he'd be secure in the recovery room and afterward in the intensive care unit for another several hours.

Sebastian figured he might as well get some rest now, stock up on the energy he'd need later. He leaped onto the couch and settled down with the television remote control.

Lady Sharon finally quit squeaking that silly toy and joined Sebastian on the couch, resting her chin on his rump. She watched his dexterity with the remote with obvious admiration.

A news bulletin was on. "General Hernando Ormegone of Balmunio has called once more for the ouster of President Eduardo Mardatia and the removal of the American naval base located in that country."

The picture switched from the announcer to General Ormegone. "Our president is no longer able to govern," the general said. "Did he not collapse at the recent state reception? Have we seen him in public since? I challenge him to come stand by my side and address the people—if he is still alive. I believe that Mardatia is dead. I believe his followers are trying to keep this secret so that they can continue to rule the country in his name. Why else would Mardatia not be seen publicly?" He smiled through thin lips. "I declare myself the leader of our country. And I dare Eduardo Mardatia to step forward and deny me—if he can. In fact, I promise my people that I will have a big surprise for them tomorrow."

The announcer came back on. "A spokesperson for President Mardatia has sent word that the president will address his people tonight at ten o'clock Eastern Standard Time, direct from the palace. This network will carry his address live."

Sebastian curled his lip, showing his bone-crushing teeth. He didn't like that general very much. After all, the people had elected their president. If they'd wanted the general, they'd have elected him, instead. He was a troublemaker.

He flipped off the television and napped. When Sebastian awoke again, Maude was coming through the door. He hadn't intended to nap so long! She fed Sebastian and Lady Sharon—dry food, of all things—and let them out in the yard awhile. Later they all sat on the couch, watching the newscast on television.

President Mardatia was sitting behind a highly polished, carved desk in a big room with velvet drapes and gold-framed portraits. "I am still your president," the translator said in English as Mardatia spoke in his native language. "I am still carrying on the business of our country. And as long as I am your president, the United States will be welcome here. I have only a slight virus."

Sebastian could see that the man had circles under his eyes and looked almost as pale as John had. That flu stuff was everywhere!

"This is the reason I have cancelled some of my public appearances," Mardatia continued. "Soon I will resume my regular schedule. One thing further. I am firing General Ormegone. The armies must no longer take orders from him. If he continues to challenge me, I shall order his arrest as an enemy of the state."

The network announcer came back on. "We could not reach General Ormegone for comment. Rumors are that he has fled the country, but we cannot confirm this."

A panel of newsmen came on to discuss the broadcast, and Maude flipped off the set. She clicked her tongue against her teeth. *"Tsk, tsk.* That Mardatia is a strong, good man, and a friend to the free world. I hope he succeeds in keeping his country from the clutches of that General Ormegone. Maybe Ormegone really has fled the country. Maybe we'll never hear from him again."

Sebastian whimpered, realizing that somehow bad men keep turning up, just when you least expect them to. And he was worried about John, too. He missed their comfortable evenings on the couch, reading, watching television. He really missed John's tender pats on the head.

Maude patted Sebastian's head reassuringly. "I know you miss John, boy. Don't worry, fellow. John's doing fine. His fever is down, and they've scheduled him for surgery tomorrow." She giggled. "You'd die laughing if you could see poor John and if you understood any of what's going on. They put him in the children's section, since they're the only other patients having tonsillectomies. Maybe we should take him a teddy bear and some jammies with feet in them."

Sebastian spread his lips in a panting grin. He was glad to hear that John was doing better. And it *was* kind of funny that he was with a bunch of kids.

He yawned, pretending he was sleepy. Soon Lady Sharon and Maude were yawning, too. The power of suggestion! Finally, everyone settled down to sleep.

The cagey canine kept his eye on the clock, and when it said midnight, he crept to the window and silently pushed the screen open, sliding to the ground. He raced toward the hospital, then crept around to the emergency entrance, which would be the only one open at that time of night. The mystery patient should be in his private room on the seventh floor by now.

The flashing lights of an ambulance reflected on his fur for a second, and he clung to shadows. Two medics jumped from the cab of the ambulance as soon as it had stopped. They rushed to open the back doors, and a third medic inside helped them to unload the patient.

Sebastian was in luck! The sheets draped over the patient reached almost to the ground, and he was able to get under the gurney and get into the hospital undetected.

While the medics and nurses were concentrating on the patient, Sebastian slipped from the emergency room and raced to the staff elevator. He scudded inside the elevator and nudged the fourth-floor button. The nurse on duty was writing on a chart and talking on the phone. She didn't even look up when he slipped from the elevator.

Doors all along the corridor were open, and the rooms were dark, except for the light spilling in from the hall. One by one, Sebastian peeked inside, looking for his human. Then he heard a familiar snore coming from 408 and stealthily crept inside.

Beds lined both side walls, and they were all occupied. Only one of the four beds revealed a shadowy form that took up its full length. Sebastian crept to it and lifted his paws onto the edge. John's face was no longer flushed. Sebastian licked him eagerly, and John stirred slightly and moaned, "Hi, boy," but didn't awaken. He didn't feel hot now. That was good.

Sebastian started to leave. The form in the next bed stirred and sat up. The child grinned broadly and waved at Sebastian. But he didn't cry out. Gratefully, Sebastian went over and licked the boy. Maybe he'd remember this as only a dream tomorrow.

Sebastian decided to use the stairwell for the three flights up to seven. He was panting heavily by the time he reached the door with the red seven on it. He peeked inside. There was a uniform at the door to room 777. Sebastian recognized him as Officer Tom Melrose. An unusual number of white-clad people were stirring through the hall. He hadn't realized such a large staff worked at night. Was it because of the mystery patient?

Sebastian spotted Officer Rosie Dunlap in a housekeeper's uniform, working undercover. But who were the others? All thoroughly checked out, he hoped.

Sebastian decided to bluff his way in this time, at least for now. He pushed the door open fully and trotted through, sniffing the floor as he went.

One of the nurses gasped. "What th—?" Her name tag said Suzie Winters, which Sebastian committed to memory.

Officer Melrose laughed. "Oh, hi, Sebastian. Got you on bomb duty?" He turned to the nurse who'd questioned the old super sleuth's presence. "It's okay, Ms. Winters. He's one of us. Detective Jones must be close by."

"But a—a *dog* in a hospital?" She shrugged.

"Well, I suppose it beats a bomb. I'll just be glad when John Doe, whoever he is, goes back to wherever he came from."

Relieved that his presence was accepted, Sebastian continued sniffing the floor while cutting his eyes this way and that, taking in all that was there.

He read the plastic name badges as he passed each nurse. Jan Storm, RN; Chris Lerner; Sidney Scrimshaw. Merle Metcalf. He committed those names to memory; he'd check their files in personnel, just in case. Dr. Payne had said they were from different floors and they might not know one another.

Sebastian continued, nose to the floor, until he got to the door to room 777. He rose on his hind legs until his eye was even with the keyhole, straining to see through the dim light. The patient stirred and turned his head toward the door. Sebastian's mouth flew open in surprise. This was no John Doe. It was President Eduardo Mardatia.

No wonder his safety was a matter of national security! If Mardatia were no longer president, General Ormegone would surely take away the U.S. air base. We wouldn't have any defense planes in that area. Did General Ormegone know that President Mardatia was here?

Wait a minute! How could President Mardatia have been speaking from the presidential palace while in this hospital, undergoing surgery? Obvi-

ously, he had been taped for the news. If the general knew that, he might try to take over Balmunio. There might be a terrible revolution. Innocent people could die. It was a good thing that Ormegone had left the country.

Oh, no! What if he'd left for the United States? What if he was coming here, to this hospital? The general had promised a big surprise tomorrow. Maybe he already knew about the president. He might be taking steps to kill him even now. The president was in grave danger.

What a bad time for his human sidekick to be sick!

5
All a Matter of Gender

The hairy hawkshaw decided to check out the files of the seventh floor staff and assure himself that they were who their badges said they were. He had an ugly suspicion about that one nurse, Merle Metcalf, whose feet were extra big. She had shifty eyes, and her legs were even hairier than his.

Sebastian ambled casually toward the stairwell door, then scooted through. He was really getting tired of those stairs!

" 'Bye, Sebastian!" Officer Melrose called out. He was a good sort.

Swiftly descending the seven flights of stairs, the stealthy Sebastian loped through the empty halls of the business section of the hospital on the first floor and entered a room filled with filing cabinets. He pawed at the file drawer marked L-M-N until it slid open, then nudged at the folders until he came to Metcalf, Merle. She definitely worked there. He clamped his teeth on the tab and pulled. The file fell to the floor, scattering its contents.

Wait a minute! What was that? It was a picture of a blond woman with light eyes. The Merle upstairs was dark haired. There were hair dyes, and

there were colored contact lenses. Maybe she had just decided to change her image. But the height! Merle Metcalf's height was listed as five feet one inch. The Merle upstairs was at least five feet eight inches tall. She was an imposter!

Sebastian felt he should check the identity of the others, too, just in case, but there wasn't time. He had to get to seven, and quickly. Every moment's delay increased the danger to President Mardatia.

Fortunately the staff elevator was on the first floor, and the doors opened as soon as Sebastian had punched the up button. Inside, he pushed the buttons for express and seven and paced back and forth as the elevator whooshed its way upward. If only he were in time.

Something terrible forced its way into his mind. Those nurses' names—Jan, Chris, Sidney—they could all be either male or female names. And Dr. Payne was not on duty now. She had not seen these people. What if *all* of them were Ormegone's men? There would be just Tom, Rosie, and himself against them.

The elevator came to an abrupt and stomach-churning stop, and the doors slid open. Merle had a tray covered with a linen napkin, and she was entering room 777.

If he was wrong, he'd be in deep trouble. If he was right, he'd be a national hero. But he'd rather be wrong for acting than wrong for doing nothing.

Sebastian made a flying leap toward Merle and sank his teeth into her ankle.

The tray flew upward, and Merle yelled, "Yeow!" She started hopping around on one foot, shouting words that Sebastian would never repeat. The voice that came out of her was two octaves lower than any woman's voice Sebastian had ever heard. *She* was definitely a *he.*

Officer Melrose quickly handcuffed the still yelling Merle. Officer Dunlap threw down her mop and pointed her gun at him with one hand while flashing her badge with the other.

Chris Lerner was also holding a gun—and a badge from the FBI. Jan Storm was holding a gun—and a badge from the CIA. And Merle was yelling something about looking in his pocket for a badge from Interpol, which was an international police organization. Wasn't *anybody* on this floor a *real* nurse?

That left only Suzie and Sidney. Suzie was the only nurse with a girl's name, and apparently the only nurse who really *was* a nurse in this hospital. While the members of the various law agencies argued over who belonged to which law enforcement agency, Sebastian turned to check on the two remaining nurses. His body tensed as he saw Sidney backing toward the elevator, pointing a gun and dragging poor, frightened Suzie. Sebastian let a low growl escape his lips as he skulked belly to the ground with teeth bared toward Sidney.

Meanwhile, Officer Melrose leaped forward to challenge Sidney and stumbled over Sebastian. In that fraction of a second, Sidney shoved Suzie toward them, stepped through the open elevator doors, and disappeared. In his wake there was only a woman's wig left on the floor.

Rosie dove for the telephone to call security downstairs. "The phone's dead!" she yelled. "The cord's been cut!"

The FBI and Interpol scrambled down the stairs, trying to reach the first floor before Sidney. The others scrambled for telephones in patients' rooms. By the time they had located a working phone and roused the switchboard operator, Sidney had escaped the hospital grounds.

Sebastian sank to the floor, humiliated. He had the awful feeling that he had just helped General Ormegone escape. President Mardatia was in more danger than ever, and it was all his fault for getting in the way when Officer Melrose tried to capture Sidney.

6
Win Some, Lose Some

Dawn was beginning to break, and Sebastian knew that there were plenty of uniforms and investigators from every branch of law enforcement available watching the seventh floor. He'd better get back to Maude's before she woke up. He didn't want her to think he'd run away and to worry John before his surgery.

Miserable that he'd accidentally cost them the capture of General Ormegone, Sebastian arrived back at Maude's humbled—and hungry. He nosed at the window screen, but it had snapped back into place. What was he going to do? He whimpered miserably.

Lady Sharon's eager face appeared at the screen. She pushed the screen forward with her forehead until the opening was wide enough for the hairy hawkshaw to slither through. He touched his nose to hers in gratitude, then settled on the couch, exhausted and disgusted.

How could he have been so stupid? He'd had his eye on the wrong suspect, Merle. Then he'd accidentally intervened with the arrest of the real culprit. He might expect the humans to muddle up.

But not Sebastian (Super Sleuth)! Lady Sharon jumped onto the couch and settled next to Sebastian, resting her chin on his head. He was too tired to argue with her.

Maude got up soon and dished the two dogs some breakfast—dry food again. Sebastian would be glad when John got home and served him all those moist, meaty surprises.

"Had a good night's sleep, huh, babies?" Maude said as she filled the water bowl. "Well, I'm going to go to the hospital. John will have his surgery in a few hours, and I want to be there when he wakes up. He'll be needing a little tender loving care by then."

Maude let Sebastian and Lady Sharon outside while she dressed, then called them inside. "You two behave while I'm gone. See you later, babies."

Babies. Sebastian wished she'd treat him with more respect. Well, he didn't respect himself right now, not after his terrible mistakes last night. He'd make them up somehow. Sebastian punched the remote control on the television. The news was on. There was no mention of the incidents at City Hospital. They were keeping it all quiet. They were probably as embarrassed as he, flashing their guns and badges at one another. At least the curious public and reporters would stay away as long as the president's presence remained a secret.

General Ormegone would surely make another

attempt on President Mardatia's life. This time Sebastian would be ready.

Sebastian waited until Maude was gone, then left through the window. Ignoring Lady Sharon's yips, he raced toward the hospital once more.

Ormegone would not use a nurse or doctor disguise again. He would be more clever. It was up to this canine to be even more clever.

At the entrance to the hospital parking lot, Sebastian paused to allow a truck to go through. A scaffold bounced precariously on top of it, and one of the hooks dangled over the side, causing sparks as it struck the concrete. These men, obviously window washers, were certainly careless with equipment that would soon be dangling them from the roof.

Sebastian trembled at the thought of hanging over the side of a building many floors above the ground, with only a chain holding him up. That was a dangerous way to make a living. He felt safer being a detective.

The window washers would need to get inside the hospital. Maybe he could get in at the same time. He trotted toward the back entrance of the building, where the window-washing truck had parked. Two men in coveralls crawled from the truck and removed the scaffold from the truck's roof. Gingerly they carried it through the service entrance, and Sebastian took that opportunity to skitter inside, hidden by the scaffold, which resembled a swing for two. Safely there, he leaped into a laundry cart, carefully peering out from beneath the pile of clothes. One of the men pushed the up button on the service elevator.

A man in white pants and a white shirt embroidered with the words APEX COMMERCIAL LAUNDERERS greeted the two window washers. "I'm only going to seven," he said. "Since you're going up to the roof, let me get on last."

They nodded their agreement and struggled to get their scaffold inside the service elevator. Then the laundryman pushed the cart with Sebastian in it onto the elevator.

Sebastian dared not even breathe for fear of being discovered. His mind was racing on, though. The laundryman said he was getting off on seven. This cart was big enough to hide just about anything you wanted to hide. Was he one of the general's men? He'd bear watching.

The man pushed the cart off the elevator and, whistling, headed toward the utility room. He was stopped right away by a uniformed officer Sebastian didn't know. The officer patted the man's clothes to be sure he wasn't carrying a weapon, then asked him to go with the officer to have his credentials checked.

At least they were being a lot more careful now. Sebastian was satisfied that no one, including the general, was going to get onto this floor. Maybe his goof-up wouldn't be too costly, after all. Maybe the general was headed back to Balmunio, where he would surely be arrested.

Everything was under control. Sebastian decided to find his way back to John's floor and see if he could find out about his human. But each entrance into the main building was blocked now. Every floor had a uniform at the stairwell door. He was not going to see John. At least the general was not going to see the president, either, not unless he could turn himself into a bird and fly through the window.

Sebastian stopped in his tracks. The window! The window washers! But they couldn't— could they?

Distraught, he raced down the stairs and out through the back entrance without regard to his possible exposure. He had to be sure.

Outside, he raced to the side of the hospital, where the president's window faced. Seven floors up, white curtains flapped through an opened window. The scaffold was directly above the window and at the roof level.

A helicopter clattered overhead, then settled on the roof. The two men in the window washer uniforms lifted a form from the scaffold and into the waiting helicopter.

Sebastian barked frantically, sounding the alarm. The helicopter lifted off the roof and headed east with President Mardatia aboard.

7
One Last Effort

As he dashed across the parking lot to get the chopper in sight once more, Sebastian saw Officer Melrose leaning out the seventh-floor window, aware that President Mardatia had been kidnapped.

He'd never be able to make Officer Melrose understand what had happened. It was up to Sebastian to find out where the kidnappers were taking President Mardatia and somehow let the authorities know.

Barking frantically, Sebastian raced around the side of the building, his eyes on the sky. There was the helicopter, skimming over trees and other buildings, and no one was paying attention to it. A white chopper landing and taking off at the hospital was a routine they were used to.

The chopper passed the edge of town, keeping a steady pace. The tiring canine loped through yards, leaped over fences, and dodged dogs defending their own turf. He turned onto a small road with trees on each side and finally collapsed, panting, as the chopper continued on its way.

When he'd caught his breath, he willed his aching muscles and sore pads to keep going, hoping to see some sign of the chopper. But what could he do if he found it? How would he lead authorities there? Who but John, who was concerned for his safety, would care enough to pursue Sebastian?

Sebastian paused to lap water from a birdbath in the front yard of a quaint cottage. Through the window he could see the light of a television set. He sneaked up to the window to peer inside. It was a special newscast.

"President Eduardo Mardatia of Balmunio, who had secretly undergone heart surgery at City Hospital, has been abducted by unknown assailants. Police surmise that he was lifted through the window of his room onto a scaffold and carried to the roof, where a waiting helicopter took him away. The uniforms of a window-washing company were found on the roof, and a stolen vehicle was located in the hospital parking lot. Authorities believe that the renegade General—"

Suddenly, the broadcast picture switched to a room with a hospital bed. It was President Mardatia. He was still alive! General Ormegone stepped in front of the camera. He spoke in his own language. At the same time, a voice translated his words into English. "Eduardo Mardatia is convalescing in my care," he said. "And I declare myself president of Balmunio. I will address you in exactly one hour, when Mardatia will resign officially."

Ormegone wouldn't harm Mardatia, at least not yet, not until the president had resigned. Ormegone would be afraid of making Mardatia a martyr to his people. There was still a chance to save him.

The general had broken into the regular broadcast. That meant he had the equipment to jam regular signals and to beam by satellite to Balmunio. He hadn't stayed on the air long enough for authorities to trace the location. But the hairy hawkshaw had a leg up on them; he knew where to look. All he had to do was find a transmitter and a flat clearing in this vicinity where a helicopter could land. Then he'd have to figure out a way to let the police know.

With renewed vigor, Sebastian galloped toward where he'd last seen the helicopter. Buildings were scattered along the road, and the trees obscured vision. As Sebastian loped past the dog pound, a chorus of barks and howls erupted. Its captives had caught his scent.

But before long he found a one-story building with a tall transmitter. It belonged to the defunct station, KZAP.

There was no helicopter in sight, but the ground showed indentations where a chopper had landed, and leaves had been scattered across a wide area. That must be the spot from which Ormegone had broadcast and where he was holding President Mardatia.

Sebastian had to be sure, though. He crept to the building and found a window opened just a crack. He forced it open farther with his nose, then crawled inside. The door to the room was closed, but he peeked through the keyhole.

There was President Mardatia. A man in a doctor's smock leaned over him, adjusting the IV and checking him. At least he was being taken care of—for now.

"It is twenty minutes until broadcast, President Ormegone," a man with a thick accent said.

Humpt! Ormegone's followers were already calling him president. Twenty minutes! Sebastian had to hurry. But how was he going to get someone to come here?

The cagey canine suddenly had an idea. As swiftly as a fox, he leaped from the building and rushed back the way he'd come.

At the dog pound, he sneaked from one cage to another, pawing at the latches until the gates swung open. He growled a warning to each dog to wait until his signal, and, grateful for their unexpected freedom, they obeyed.

When the last latch fell useless, Sebastian (Super Sleuth) yelped, and barking, yowling dogs followed his lead, down the driveway, past the dogcatcher's truck, and down the road.

The startled dogcatcher ran out the front door, shouting to someone inside. "Dial nine-one-one.

We're going to need help!" He leaped into his truck and gave chase, but the dogs—tall ones, short ones, fat ones, and thin ones—were spurred onward by Sebastian's barks of encouragement.

Sirens sounded in the distance. Perfect! His timing, if his inner clock was right (and wasn't it always?) would get them there just as the broadcast was beginning.

Dogs circled the KZAP building, following Sebastian's lead. They barked and howled, and they scratched at doors and windows. The ruckus was even more than Sebastian had hoped for, and the front door to the building flew open.

At Sebastian's signaling woof, the dogs rushed into the building, knocking Ormegone's assistant to the ground and startling Ormegone, who'd just begun his broadcast.

But what if the police didn't arrive in time? Sebastian rose to his full height and shoved against the second camera with all his might. For everyone to see, the camera with its KZAP call letters printed on the side came into view. That would leave no doubt where this hideaway was. Unfortunately, the hairy hawkshaw was in full camera view, too.

One more yelping signal and the dogs scattered, many heading home to some anxious boy or girl. As the squad cars pulled to a screeching stop outside, Sebastian slipped through a window and dis-

appeared into the shrubbery to observe.

Moments later, the dogcatcher and police tumbled into the building to find not dogs, but instead the president of Balmunio and his captors.

Soon an ambulance arrived to return President Mardatia to the hospital, and Ormegone and his aides were handcuffed and loaded into squad cars. When they were finished serving time in the U.S. for kidnapping and illegally entering the country, they would no doubt face charges of treason in Balmunio.

Sebastian trotted the long way back to Maude's, pleased with the outcome. The old sleuth hound had vindicated himself. Now all he had to worry about was John.

He managed to slip back into the house before Maude returned. She was so happy that she gave them extra helpings of hamburger. "John's just fine, and he's coming home tomorrow," she said, rubbing Sebastian the length of his aching back.

The next day, Sebastian wiggled with happiness as John was wheeled to Maude's car. The stub of his tail twitched, and he licked John's face again and again.

John laughed. "You know, I was watching the news last night, and I saw a dog that looked just like Sebastian leading the raid on Ormegone. It *wasn't* Sebastian, *was—*"

Maude giggled. "Sebastian? Solving a kidnapping? Oh, John, be reasonable!"

At John's apartment, Maude helped him settle comfortably, promising to return later with some broth and some fudge ripple ice cream, which was Sebastian's favorite.

John pulled the covers up to his chin, and Sebastian sat close by, his chin resting on the edge of the bed. He gazed lovingly at his recuperating partner in crime-fighting. "And another thing," John said. "I had this funny sensation that Sebastian came to see me in the hospital. He *didn't, did* he?"

Maude shook with laughter as she took her car keys from her purse. "That lazy hound wasn't off my couch, except to eat. You had a dream, silly." She closed the door behind her, still chuckling.

Sebastian's lips parted in a panting grin. Hadn't she ever heard that dreams could come true?

He gave his human another warm, wet sleep-tight puppy kiss on the cheek, then settled down on the rug beside the bed.

It was time to rest up for the next case.